W9-DEF-823

ALL BUT LOVE

Ann Howard White

A KISMET® Romance

METEOR PUBLISHING CORPORATION
Bensalem, Pennsylvania

To Anne, Deb, Pat, and Sandra, for their invaluable advice and encouragement;

Nancy, for pushing me in the right direction at the right time;

Catherine Carpenter and Meteor Publishing, for giving me the opportunity;

And Ed, for never losing faith.

ANN HOWARD WHITE

Ann Howard White discovered the romance genre straight out of three long, tedious years of law school—and instantly became a fan. After voraciously reading literally thousands of books, she decided to draw on her experiences as wife of a professional and mother of three, her love of people, and her involvement in civic and professional groups, combine them with her active imagination and passion for writing, and create her own romantic stories.

_____ ONE _____

She wasn't his type.

Mark Garrett shifted slightly in the first-class seat of the Boeing 757 to better study the woman's profile. The late-afternoon trip from Atlanta to St. Croix was long and tiring, and there were still a couple of hours to go. To make matters worse, his seat didn't quite accommodate his broad shoulders and larger-than-average frame. His seat belt, kept loosely buckled in anticipation of predicted air turbulence, further restricted him. God, how he hated restraints. Restless, he'd begun to check out the other passengers. That's when he'd first noticed the woman occupying the seat across the aisle.

So why did his eyes keep returning to her? And why did each look draw him back? She sat angled toward the empty window seat beside her, providing him a clear view of graceful neck and contoured cheek as she concentrated on a book. He could see enough to judge that she wasn't beautiful—couldn't even be classified as particularly pretty. Her mousey-brown hair was scraped back severely into an exacting hairstyle, securely anchored by some sort of large clasp. Lord, Mark thought distastefully, that alone was enough to turn him off.

Her clothing wasn't much better, he decided as his eyes slid over her attire. At best, it could be described as utilitarian—and plain. A nondescript voluminous white blouse seemed to engulf her thin torso. What covered the lower half of her body was obscured from his view by the armrest and the fact that she was turned slightly away from him.

But there was a serenity about her, an outward confidence, that didn't quite conceal an underlying vulnerability.

Mark restlessly shifted again, stretching his long jeans-clad legs out beside the aisle seat in front of him, carelessly stacking one ankle over the other. His eyes sharpened as he intensified his scrutiny. There was an elusive quality about her that made a man wonder what lay hidden under that cool facade, challenged a man to delve beneath the surface. He wondered fleetingly if she were aware she had that effect on his sex.

No, she wasn't his usual type.

Of course, he admitted grudgingly, he couldn't say much for his "usual" type. The few relationships since his disastrous marriage had been brief, physical, and unemotional. Those occasional women tended to be model perfect, with beautiful faces and sexy bodies, possessing all the trappings of success and epitomizing all that had been lacking in his youth. Their kind wasn't found in the slums where he'd grown up, surrounded by poverty. They were sleek and sophisticated, worldwise and knew the score—and expected nothing from him but a good time and physical pleasure.

And were not vulnerable.

Mark snorted derisively to himself. Certainly the

woman sitting across from him didn't fit the profile. Unfortunately, his type also tended to be shallow. It wasn't that he didn't believe beauty and substance could go together. It just hadn't been his experience. Until recently it hadn't mattered, in fact had been just the way he wanted it. No complications and no commitments. But lately . . .

No, she definitely wasn't his type. Still, something about her intrigued him.

Feeling as though she were being minutely dissected, Dr. Catherine Jayne Chambers abruptly slanted her head toward the man seated across the aisle and looked straight into a pair of gray eyes so piercingly clear they seemed unfathomable. The impact of his stare was breathtaking, and she couldn't disentangle her gaze from his. Her lethargy, induced by the plane's droning engines, instantly dissipated. She was now wide awake.

He exuded cocky sexuality from the tilt of his ebony-haired head to the insolent angle of his lithe body sprawled in the seat. An aura of success emanated from him that was at sharp variance with an elusive ruffian quality. Though he was casually dressed, his clothing hinted at designer labels, and money—lots of it.

There was a quiet waiting about him. It seemed to forewarn a careful observer that, if cornered, he would be dangerous.

Two thoughts accosted her simultaneously. Not only was this man compellingly attractive, with a cynical magnetism reaching far beyond his storm-colored eyes, but he was also accustomed, she was certain, to obtaining whatever he went after. As if he could read her mind and wanted to emphasize the point, his eyes refused to release hers. They continued to delve into her. The effect sent shock waves of awareness scattering along her spine to settle low in her belly, causing her heart to begin a heavy cadence against her ribs that had little to do with fear and a lot to do with something much more basic.

She was only vaguely conscious of the smile that played at one corner of his unyieldingly masculine mouth. When her stare didn't falter, his slowly took on a mocking light.

Just when the tension had stretched to monumental proportions, his gaze abruptly moved to the young girl seated beside him.

Catherine expelled a shuddering breath and watched, fascinated, as the man's demeanor changed. His face softened and he bent to look at what the child was showing him. The contrast between his earlier cynicism and this tentative gentleness was startling. But his apparent awkwardness with the child puzzled Catherine. With a certainty she couldn't account for, she knew this man's defiant self-confidence was rarely shaken.

"Do you like it?" Catherine could just make out what the girl asked as she held up a piece of paper for his inspection. The rest of the conversation was lost to the steady hum of the turbines.

They must be father and daughter, Catherine surmised because of the strong family resemblance. Both had the same striking gray eyes. She could sense the love between them. Though restrained, it radiated from the child's face as she hesitantly looked up at the man, and was returned in his gentled features. He carefully studied the paper the girl had given him, her desire for his approval evident in her anxious expression.

Something painful squeezed within Catherine, and she, too, awaited his reaction. Memories of a lonely childhood crept to the surface. As she recalled vain attempts to please her unyielding father, she empathized with this child. But Catherine had been destined to fail. Gaining her father's approval had been impossible, and the smallest affection had been a rarity. She hoped this child was luckier.

When his smile came, Catherine breathed a sigh of relief and felt an unexpected wave of tenderness toward the man.

Somewhat perturbed by her reactions, Catherine mentally shook herself. This was not like her. To sit here *ogling* this particular man was completely out of character. The fact that he was accompanied by a child made him, intuition warned her, no less a threat to her emotional defenses.

As she was deliberately forcing her attention back to her abandoned book, the huge plane suddenly vibrated, then lurched, jerking Catherine against the restraining seat belt. She wasn't given a chance to catch her breath before she felt the plane plunge downward, with a violence alarming in its intensity, into a headlong free fall.

Catherine watched in fascinated horror as in nightmarish slow motion loose pieces of luggage and belongings were flung about the cabin, inflicting indiscriminate damage on person and thing. Shrieks, mixed with muffled groans, punctuated by sobs, assaulted her ears. She thought she heard a child scream, but couldn't be sure in the confusion. The frenzied roller-coaster ride ended with a savage jolt within what must have been mere seconds but what to her seemed an eternity, throwing passengers and possessions already in chaos into further jeopardy.

Dazed by the sharp impact of the plane settling out of its dive, Catherine required a few moments to orient herself. She mentally ran a checklist of her body and, finding no injuries, waited for the adrenaline rush to subside.

"Sorry about the unscheduled carnival ride, folks," came the captain's disembodied voice over the plane's intercom, but his weak attempt at levity fell flat. "The worst of the turbulence should be behind us now." Catherine half listened to something about air pockets and his plea to stay seated and keep seat belts fastened. "If there's a doctor in the house, we'd sure appreciate your assistance should it be needed."

Catherine's attention instantly shifted to the man and child across from her. He'd released his seat belt, blatantly ignoring the captain's warning, and was bending over the little girl in the window seat beside him.

The sight of her deathly-still form galvanized Catherine into action and her cool professional efficiency took over. She fumbled with her seat belt, rationalizing that the captain *had* asked for medical assistance. Standing on less-than-steady legs, she grabbed her medical bag from the overhead compartment and moved to the man's side.

She dropped the bag on the floor close at hand and bent over his right shoulder to see past him to the small inert figure. As she reached for the child, an unsteady, powerful hand clamped over Catherine's forearm halting her movement.

"What the hell are you doing?"

Catherine's eyes sought and encountered savage gray ones. Her ability to calm frantic family members and hysterical patients was well known within the Atlanta medical community. In fact, it was considered almost a gift, as the hectic pace of her pediatric surgical practice demonstrated. At the moment, however, she had some doubt of being as successful with this man.

"Please," she urged, instilling the word with what she hoped was persuasive authority, "I'm a doctor. Let me check her."

Time seemed to elongate, as did the restrained urgency in the man. He did not relinquish his unyielding grip on her arm nor on her attention. Catherine withstood the cold analysis of his glittering eyes until an awareness of the calloused strength in his hand seeped into her consciousness. With it came an unreasonable urge to snatch her arm free. Before she could act on the impulse, his hand dropped away, leaving her with the indelible impression that he'd made some irrevocable decision.

Reeling from the urgency transmitted by his fingers, Catherine took an involuntary half-step back, grabbing the armrest to steady herself. *Well, the man certainly isn't one to waste words*, she observed silently.

He rose jerkily and moved aside to allow her access to the motionless form slumped in the far seat. But not before she'd glimpsed the anguish he quickly camouflaged.

"Thank you," she said reassuringly before taking his vacated seat.

Catherine concentrated on the child who rested at an awkward angle, held upright by the seat belt. Swiftly but with exacting care she searched for indications of fracture. Finding none, she unbuckled the seat belt. The middle armrest had been raised, enabling Catherine to lay her prone and facilitate the examination.

Simultaneously monitoring a strong, steady pulse, Catherine rapidly inventoried the girl's face and body. Though pale, her overall color was good. A darkening contusion on the small forehead was the only outward evidence of injury, and Catherine's meticulous fingers delicately palpated, eliciting a faint whimper from her small patient. At the sound, Catherine relaxed the frown marring her own forehead; at least the child was not deeply unconscious.

A flight attendant's voice suddenly intruded. "Is she hurt badly?"

Catherine did not spare a glance. "I haven't finished examining her."

"You're a doctor?"

"Yes."

"Oh, good." The woman's voice held a wealth of relief. "I'll get back to you as soon as we know if anyone else is injured." Without waiting for Catherine to respond, she rushed away.

Catherine groped in her bag for an otoscope, then carefully lifted each of the child's eyelids to check pupil reflexes. Finding them equal and responsive to light— another promising indication—Catherine released a tightly held breath.

All the while her brain methodically ticked off the necessary medical procedures, she was keenly aware of the man's presence that seemed to loom over her. Catherine had never failed effectively to block out everything and everyone save her patient. Until now.

But she couldn't forget the ruthlessly suppressed anguish she'd witnessed earlier in this outwardly invincible man.

"What's her name?" she asked. In order to see his face, Catherine had to tilt her head at an uncomfortable angle. He stood partially in the aisle, one strong hand gripping the overhead compartment to steady himself against the continued pitch and roll of the plane. A scar on his left cheek accentuated the severity of his not-quite-perfect features. She could almost believe him relaxed but for the subtle tension belying that assumption.

"Beth." The word was raw.

Catherine repeated the name, her voice firm but gentle.

Beth's answering moan was stronger.

Acutely attuned to the man's apprehension, Catherine heard him mutter, more to himself than to her, "She's okay." It was said flatly—a statement, not a question, as if by saying it he could make it so.

A tiny pleat formed between Catherine's finely arched brows, and she turned on the seat to face him. It was time to tell him her preliminary findings, but she felt unprepared for the inevitable confrontation. Her gaze resolutely climbed hard thighs encased in denim, skimmed over a narrow waist, measured the width of powerful shoulders, and came to rest just short of penetrating eyes. "She's sustained a moderately severe blow to her head, probably from hitting the bulkhead during the turbulence. Nothing appears to be broken, but she *is* unconscious."

He made no comment, the intensity of his silence commanding her to continue.

Catherine raised her eyes the last few millimeters to connect with his, and her heart gave a strange little lurch inside her chest. "Her physical and neurological signs are good."

He expelled an expletive. "What the hell does that mean?"

When this man *did* choose to speak, Catherine decided, his vocabulary left something to be desired. "She responds to voice and light," she carefully explained. "Her heartbeat is steady. All are positive signs. But," she added, holding his narrowed gaze with some difficulty, "she has at least a mild concussion. I can't be certain what else." Knowing full well he would not complacently accept her next words, she hesitated infinitesimally. "It's possible she could have internal injuries."

Even in the dim cabin light, she could see his face

blanch under his dark tan. "Injuries?" The word was wiped as clean of emotion as was his expression.

"I can't tell without lab tests and x-rays," Catherine clarified, softening the words as best she could. She hated this part of medicine, this searching for the least traumatic way to deliver less than optimistic news. "Or at the very least, until she regains consciousness and I can talk with her."

She'd known it wasn't going to be easy. This man would take nothing lying down. His demeanor suggested that he was on intimate terms with adversity and didn't flinch from meeting it head-on. She had no doubt that where someone he cared about was concerned, it would be a no-holds-barred battle. Not by so much as a muscle twitch did he reveal the struggle she sensed beneath his deceptively calm exterior.

Mark controlled his feeling of helplessness by steely determination. *She has competent hands*, he observed distractedly. Her fingers were long and slender, tipped with softly rounded nails bare of polish. The latent ability contained in them registered in the forefront of his mind. On a deeper level he filed away the impression of fragility—and the absence of jewelry.

When he said nothing further, she held out her hand almost in a gesture of supplication. "Let me have your coat."

He shrugged out of the soft denim jacket, passing it to her with hands that still trembled slightly. It was warm with his body heat, and the small intimacy caused her heart to skitter.

Catherine wrapped Beth in the coat, then stood, indicating that he should take her place. His imposing six-foot-plus height gave little room to maneuver, leaving Catherine no alternative but to brush against his broad chest as she eased past him into the aisle. The humming awareness that sang through her was more than a little unsettling.

Steady, girl, Catherine warned herself. It wasn't like her to let a man—any man—breach her defenses.

Catherine reached across him and carefully positioned Beth on his lap. "Keep her quiet and warm," she said briskly, summoning her most professional tone. "Talk to her. Hearing a familiar voice will help bring her around. That's all we can do for the moment."

"Yeah, well, I don't think she'll consider my voice all that familiar," he told her bleakly.

The grim statement surprised Catherine. "I know this is hard on you." She deliberated a moment. She was aware that giving out premature hope wasn't wise, but something compelled her to add quietly, "Try not to worry. Everything indicates she'll be fine."

Her words appeared to lessen the tightly coiled tension in him.

Annoyed at allowing this lapse in objectivity, Catherine ordered herself to run a clinical eye over him. His face remained expressionless, his shirt-clad torso partially hidden by the child he held protectively in his arms. "Are you hurt?"

"No," he answered curtly. Her renewed impersonal air irritated him for some reason. "Thanks for taking care of my daughter." He tenderly repositioned Beth on his lap, then extended his right hand. "Mark Garrett." The reciprocal inquiry was implicit in his tone.

His hand was steady now, Catherine noted, making her aware that he was once again under iron control. She wanted to ignore the gesture but knew, as his hand enveloped hers, there was no graceful way she could. His was warm and commanding and touched much more than her palm and fingers—threatened a spot deep within she kept painstakingly guarded. "Dr. Chambers," she responded, feeling inexplicably as if she were revealing some dark secret.

Let's not lose control here, she admonished herself firmly. All she had to do was remain professional. She did it every day, routinely. Surely she could do it now.

The flight attendant's return dissolved the spell. "How're we doing?"

Catherine freed her hand and gratefully transferred her attention to the woman. "She's resting comfortably for the moment. Anyone else injured?"

"Some bumps and bruises. Nothing serious, thank God, but would you mind taking a look?"

As Catherine bent to retrieve her bag, Mark's strong fingers caught hold of her arm. "Are you all right? Can you handle this by yourself?" he asked, gesturing in the general direction of the other passengers.

Catherine bristled slightly. "I appreciate your concern, Mr. Garrett, but I believe I can manage it."

"You're sure?"

She regarded him a moment but could detect no hint of condescension, only thinly veiled frustration. When he glanced down at his small daughter, she understood, with unanticipated clarity, that he was torn between his need to stay with Beth and a desire to help her, that his frustration was from his inability to assist the person who'd come to his child's aid.

Catherine wondered vaguely why she wasn't more affronted by his subtle, albeit well-meaning, challenge to her medical capability. And why, instead, she felt oddly touched by his concern. She was unaccustomed to a man looking out for her. In fact, most men she encountered felt uncomfortable around a woman who was also a doctor.

Her voice softened. "Yes, I'm sure, but thanks. Keep Beth warm. And talk to her."

"Yeah, right."

The bleak reply slowed Catherine's departure. She clutched the seatback to steady herself as much from the internal upheaval assaulting her as from the plane's drunken adjustment to continued air turbulence. Before following the hovering flight attendant, she quietly added, "I'll be back as soon as I can."

The lady doctor looked too delicate to carry the heavy responsibilities of a medical practice, Mark decided.

Watching her make her way back up the aisle toward him a short while later, he was acutely reminded of her fragility. Dark sherry-brown eyes reflected her fatigue. Her vulnerability, only hinted at earlier, was pronounced now, and he was more than a little perturbed by the fierce protectiveness besieging him. Remembering his immediate trust in her ability to care for his daughter didn't help allay his disturbing thoughts. Strange, he reflected cynically. Except maybe where Beth was concerned, those emotions were alien to him.

"How is she?" Catherine asked as she eased past Mark Garrett's legs to sit on the edge of the seat. There was only a cramped space remaining beside him and Beth's small body, and Catherine tried to avoid as much physical contact with him as possible. It must be his superior height and powerful size, she rationalized, that unsettled her.

Before he had time to answer, Beth opened her eyes, focusing blearily on Catherine.

"Well, hello there," Catherine greeted. "I'm Dr. Chambers, but I let my very best patients call me CJ." All the while her voice soothed, her hands discreetly assessed Beth for injuries. "You gave us quite a scare. Do you think you can sit up so I can check you over?"

As Mark Garrett helped his daughter into a partially upright position, Catherine's eyes connected with his. Her heart contracted at the undisguised relief on his harsh face. She had to fight to keep from revealing the intensity of her reaction as she directed her attention back to Beth. "How do you feel?"

"My head hurts a little bit." Beth's voice was groggy.

"Do you hurt anywhere else? Feel nauseated?"

Beth gave a negative shake to both questions.

Catherine offered a silent prayer of thanks, then, to evaluate how lucid the child was, asked, "Can you tell me your name?"

Beth smiled weakly at this and nodded. "It's Beth."

As his daughter's response grew stronger, Mark felt the tightly knotted muscles in his stomach begin to loosen their grip. He hugged Beth gingerly, careful not to hurt her. "Hi, princess."

"What happened?" Beth asked, still a little dazed.

Mark pulled his daughter onto his lap. "You bumped your head when the plane hit an air pocket—kind of like a roller-coaster ride. A rough one." The words were raspy, and he had to clear his throat before continuing. "You doing okay?"

"I guess so, 'cept for my head." More alert now, Beth switched her solemn gray gaze to Catherine. "CJ's a funny name. What does it mean?"

"It stands for Catherine Jayne. You don't think CJ's better? Most of the kids I work with think it's easier to remember."

Beth considered this guilelessly, then gave a doubtful shrug. "Do you have a little girl?"

Catherine momentarily recoiled from the answer,

concentrating instead on the fact that Beth's alert question indicated any confusion from the injury was dissipating. After a moment she cautiously allowed the memory to surface. Only a dull ache remained to remind her of the once-slashing pain caused by the loss of her baby. A little girl who would have been only a little older than Beth was now.

"No, not one of my very own," Catherine replied in a husky voice, forcing a smile at the innocent query. "But lots of them come to see me. I try to make them feel better." She was oddly gratified to see a small smile lighten Beth's somber face.

The echo of pain in Catherine's words didn't escape Mark, and he experienced an illogical urge to banish it. "So, she's going to be okay?" He knew he'd succeeded as he witnessed Catherine again raise her professional shield.

"Her headache needs to be monitored for the next twenty-four hours—"

But the plane's captain cut short her clinical recitation. "Doctor," he said, stopping beside them, "I want to thank you for all your help."

"Luckily there wasn't much I needed to do. You and your crew are certainly well trained in emergency procedures." Smiling warmly, she added, "We should thank you for keeping us in the air. And for having remarkably few injuries."

The captain's smile broadened, and he ran a practiced glance over her. "Not only a talented doctor, but charming as well."

Catherine didn't respond to the compliment. "I'm glad I was here to help."

Mark's eyes narrowed. He wasn't used to humility in women. Experience had taught him that they expected praise and compliments, deserved or not, particularly from men.

The captain nodded in Beth's direction. "How's the little girl?"

Catherine touched Beth's shoulder in a spontaneous gesture of comfort. "I think she's going to be okay, but she needs x-rays and other tests as soon as we land."

"And how soon will that be, Captain?" There was a sharp edge to Mark's softly spoken question that cut off further conversation.

The captain checked his watch. "About an hour." Directing a mock salute and wink at Catherine, he left them to continue his rounds.

"Are you going to give me the . . . x-rays?" Beth asked in a small voice, once the pilot had departed.

Catherine was impressed by Beth's stoic composure. Any other child her age, which she estimated to be six or seven, would likely be in tears by now. Having witnessed the father's iron control, Catherine decided it must run in the family.

"Honey, there are lots of nice people at the hospital who will take good care of you."

"But I don't *want* them to take care of me. Please, I want you to. I like you."

Mark realized that the doctor couldn't possibly know how uncharacteristic his daughter's request was. He felt an unreasonable resentment and a gut-deep ache that he couldn't supply Beth's needs. "It looks like you've made a conquest." His tone was sardonic. "Can you continue her care on the island?"

His metallic gaze held a challenging glint, and Catherine sensed an unfathomable emotion in him. Again she felt her defenses threatened and instinctively recognized the potential danger to her own emotional well-being.

"It . . . would be difficult. I'm not on staff at the island hospital," she hedged. "It would be better if one of their doctors continued Beth's treatment." The excuse was weak. She was aware that in an emergency situation wide latitude could be extended to outside medical personnel. And besides she would be staying with the hospital's chief-of-staff.

Beth's small hand reached out to her. "Please, say you will."

Mark didn't understand his compelling need to assure that his daughter—that *he*—would see this woman again. He resented the thought. "Come now, Dr. Chambers, surely you wouldn't desert your patient?" His tone was just short of mocking.

"I'll show you my pictures if you'll take care of me," Beth interjected in her small, quiet voice. "I'll even draw one for you."

"I'd love to see your drawings." Catherine decided to play for time, self-preservation urging her to reinforce her defenses. "Do you have any with you?"

Beth searched for her scattered pictures, finding them crushed between the two seats. "Here they are," she said, and shyly pushed them into Catherine's hands.

The untutored simplicity of the drawings did not disguise her natural talent. "Why, these are beautiful." Catherine leafed through the rumpled papers a second time. "I'm impressed. You must take lessons."

Beth appeared both pleased and sheepish. "Daddy doesn't think I should waste my time on drawing pictures. So I just do it for fun. Do you really like them?" The words came all in one breath as if she needed to get them out before losing her nerve.

Wondering why something so innocuous should

cause dissension between father and daughter, Catherine looked into eyes serious beyond their owner's young years and answered sincerely. "Yes, I really like them." She was rewarded by a pleased smile but could see that Beth was beginning to tire. "Why don't you rest now and we'll talk some more later, okay?"

"Okay." Though Beth couldn't hide her yawn, she complied with reluctance.

When the child had dozed off, Catherine faced Mark squarely. "Do you actually believe this is a waste of time?" she asked in an incredulous whisper. "I don't pretend to be an expert, but even I can see she has talent. Why would you want to thwart that?"

Mark's mouth tightened with displeasure at being questioned on a subject he felt already settled. He also didn't like the overwhelming sensation that he should, no, not should—*must*—defend himself to this woman. "Thwart," he repeated, testing the word. "Very quaintly put. I have nothing against her drawing, but it's way down on my list of what's important in life."

Catherine sensed an underlying warning in the mild statement. Still, something drove her to persist. "Art lessons don't have to be the most important thing in her life, but a gift like hers should be encouraged. Have you looked into it? What does your wife think?"

He gritted his teeth. He'd had enough interference in Beth's unbringing to last him a lifetime.

"My wife is dead," he stated succinctly. "I didn't realize you were a specialist in child psychology—or art either, for that matter." His voice was quiet but hard-edged. "Just make her well, Doctor. I'll take care of the rest." He didn't add that he'd experienced first-hand the consequences when art became all-consuming in a person's life. And that he'd make damned sure it didn't happen to Beth.

Catherine felt her face flush with embarrassment, but she couldn't be insulted. He was right. Her comments were out of line. *Lord, what in heaven's name is the matter with me?* Where was her professional detachment? Her policy was never to interfere in a patient's personal life unless it had a direct bearing on his or her health. That certainly wasn't the case here. And she definitely shouldn't be interfering in the personal life of this particular man or his child.

Catherine squared her shoulders and forced herself to hold Mark Garrett's censuring stare. "You're right. I'm sorry. This is none of my business." Or at least it shouldn't be. But she couldn't shake the unexplainable affinity she felt for this child.

Mark watched her retreat. She was an intriguing contradiction, he reflected, efficiently cool in a medical emergency, but easily flustered in a personal confrontation. And the contradiction was having a disturbing effect on him.

He prided himself on keeping his carnal cravings under strict control, but he was having difficulty subduing the primitive hunger gripping him. He wanted this woman. But far more, he wanted to become intimately familiar with all her carefully guarded facets.

The strength of the yearning shook him to the core before he hastily reined it in. Well, what the hell, he resolved, he was used to going after what he wanted. He hadn't clawed his way out of the inner-city slums by being timid.

And he seldom failed to achieve his objective.

"You're evading the question, Doctor." Mark returned to his original request. It was time to try a little strategy, he decided. "Will you continue Beth's care?"

The sensation of being cornered pushed at Catherine. "It's not that simple. I'm not sure I can—"

"I didn't ask it you *can*," he interrupted, his voice smooth, "but rather if you *will*." At her wary look, Mark silently acknowledged his satisfaction at unsettling this woman. He liked ruffling her composure.

He intended to do a lot more.

"Well, what do you say? I might even be receptive to your meddling with the way I raise my daughter."

"I've already apologized, Mr. Garrett. There's no need to rub it in. What you do or don't do is none of my concern." But a niggling suspicion told her that wasn't going to be the case.

"That's not an answer, Dr. Chambers." Something in his expression taunted her. "Think of this as an experiment. Can you take care of Beth's medical needs, convince me that art lessons have merit—" there was a pause pregnant with provocation "—and still keep your mask in place?"

"I don't know what you're talking about, Mr. Garrett." She was beginning to feel a bit desperate. He seemed capable of detecting her carefully guarded weaknesses. And she found it more than a little disconcerting.

"Don't you?" The dare lay quiet in his words.

And it wasn't lost on Catherine. It made her angry. But something more, it made her want to take on the challenge—she who had learned by bitter lesson to avoid all but professional associations with men.

She raised her chin decisively. "If the hospital will agree, I'll see to Beth's care."

She deliberately ignored the rest of the challenge.

TWO

Mark strode to a halt in front of Catherine where she knelt beside the child on the airport tarmac. "They want to take Beth to the hospital in an ambulance," he clipped out. "Some bullsh—" He caught himself midword, suddenly aware that Beth was listening, then amended, "Garbage about airline regulations." His intolerance of the situation was palpable, his objection to being dependent on others blatant in his stance.

He waited while Catherine finished adjusting the blanket over Beth's shoulders. As she straightened, his gaze flicked over her, again noticing her fatigue. She was shivering despite the balmy tropical night, the gauzy fabric of her blouse and skirt apparently doing little to stave off the chill of delayed reaction. Her hair, loosened now from its repressive topknot, hung in soft tendrils and swirls around her face and neck. Its gold and auburn highlights, accented by the glaring runway lights, softened her features and made Mark question how he'd ever thought it dull.

Suppressing a curse at his errant thoughts, he sought

to temper his words. "I'd rather take her, unless you think an ambulance is necessary." He shifted impatiently, waiting for her decision.

Catherine was beginning to identify this abrasive manner as typical when Mark Garrett encountered any situation beyond his control. Rubbing her own arms for warmth, she looked around at the milling passengers awaiting transportation and considered the options. At the moment, Beth was exhibiting no residual effects from the blow to her head. Even so, it might be a while before she could be transported to the hospital. Catherine was conscious of the apprehension in the little girl huddling under the blanket beside her.

"I agree," she said after a moment. "You could get her there faster and with less distress."

Mark nodded, satisfied with her answer.

"But I don't think the airline will let you," she felt obligated to add.

Genuine amusement lifted one corner of his hard mouth. "Ah, but they will," he assured her, "if you know the right person to convince."

His unexpected humor, though tinged with cynicism, did odd things to her pulse rate. As she watched him head with long ground-eating strides toward the small island terminal she didn't doubt his success for a second and sympathized with the poor unsuspecting airline official.

Feeling that she'd been given a reprieve, Catherine again knelt beside Beth and pulled her close. This could be just what was needed to release her from the impetuous promise she'd made on the plane. By the time she reached the hospital, Beth's care would be in the hands of other doctors. Her services would no longer be required. It was for the best, she told herself. She didn't want—certainly didn't need—this kind of involvement.

But that didn't stop the small hollow ache somewhere in the region of her heart.

"Get in."

The order startled Catherine out of her troublesome thoughts, and she focused on Mark Garrett as he leaned over and opened the passenger door of a remarkably dusty Jeep. She'd been so caught up in her thoughts that she hadn't noticed its approach amid all the other confusion on the runway. When she made no move to obey his terse command, he was out of the vehicle and around the hood in seconds.

"I said, get in." This time he accompanied the words with firm yet surprisingly gentle hands as he pulled Catherine to her feet, then effortlessly lifted Beth into his arms. Before Catherine could demur, Mark herded her into the Jeep and placed Beth on her lap.

"I have to stay here in case I'm needed." Even to her own ears, the attempt to instill her voice with authority fell short.

The look Mark threw at her was skeptical. His gaze swept over her, again taking in her exhaustion. "What you need," he suggested mildly, "is a keeper." He slammed her door for emphasis, then rounded the Jeep to the driver's side.

Avoiding the manual gearshift while arranging a sleepy Beth more comfortably on her lap proved to be somewhat awkward. Good heavens, she thought in exasperation, even with transmissions the man had to be in control. She wondered if this bit of knowledge shouldn't tell her something.

He slid behind the wheel, then carefully enunciated as if explaining to someone a bit slow. "You're dead on your feet." He shoved the four-wheel drive into gear and began cautiously maneuvering around the assembled ambulances and other emergency vehicles before continuing. "You've done your bit. Someone else can take over now. Nobody, not even you, Dr. Chambers, is indispensable."

The mild sarcasm rankled, although Catherine couldn't fault his logic. He was right, she was wiped out. The crisis during the flight, following on the heels of a late night in emergency surgery before leaving Atlanta, had left her drained. She was well aware that a doctor should not practice medicine when this tired. Still, perversely, she didn't want to yield to him.

"Thank you for pointing that out, Mr. Garrett." Her retort was saccharine sweet.

Flicking his eyes to Catherine, he added, softly, "Your place is with this patient—or have you forgotten your promise?"

Her earlier thoughts of defection echoed in her head, making her defensive. "No, I have not." She'd ignore him for now, she decided, laying her head against the headrest and closing her eyes. She ought to be incensed at his domineering actions but couldn't muster the energy. When she wasn't so tired she'd sort it all out. Acquiescing silently that she'd let him have this small victory, she concentrated on the tropical night sounds racing past the open Jeep windows.

For weeks she'd been looking forward to this vacation and a long visit with Steve. She smiled inwardly thinking of her old friend and colleague. He was probably at the hospital right now, since he spent more time there than at his home. Steve Dalton could always be depended upon to put things into perspective. And right now she needed that badly.

After a few minutes Catherine opened her eyes a crack until she could just make out the contours of Mark's granite-hard features illuminated by the muted dashboard light. The faint glow darkened his hair to demon black. He was only passably handsome, she decided. And she'd almost convinced herself that his looks were further diminished by the scar on his left cheek. Even so, she grudgingly conceded, the man must be accustomed to women falling all over him. Probably took it as his due. The waspish thought surprised her.

She studied the silhouetted muscle in his right jaw as it ticked rhythmically. The intangible aura of leashed power about him challenged her on some primitive level, and she felt the swell of sexual awareness like a hot tide. Its magnitude was unnerving, and she struggled to tamp it down. *I must be more tired than I realized*. She definitely needed to get some rest—like maybe for a week . . . like maybe for the next decade!

She'd learned in her thirty-five years to observe men with an almost clinical analysis. She could appreciate their physical attributes on a purely detached level, never allowing her emotions to become engaged. It was as instinctive as it was self-protective. Except for Steve, she dealt with men only when absolutely necessary in the course of her medical practice, and as little as possible all other times.

To her growing misgiving, Mark Garrett, it seemed, was to be the exception.

In his peripheral vision, Mark could make out Catherine's hand absently stroking Beth's back and arm. *She's not even aware she's a toucher*. She did it reflexively to reassure and comfort. He speculated fleetingly if she realized how seductive that could be to a man like him—to someone whose life had been barren of such comforting gestures. What would it be like, he wondered, to be on the receiving end of her small, innocent touches?

Growling under his breath, he tightened his grip on

the steering wheel. Who was he fooling? The world was made up of two kinds of people. Those who were loved, and those who loved. Long ago he realized which category he fit. He chose not to be in either.

His interest in this woman annoyed him. It didn't make sense. He didn't need an entanglement with an uptight, meddling female.

So why had he insisted she continue Beth's care? Hell, he hadn't simply insisted, he'd done little short of coercing her! And for what? *Lust* came the answer from some perverted corner of his mind. He shook his head, as if to dislodge the idea. For months he'd been too busy for a sexual relationship. Obviously too long.

This woman seemed to go out of her way to ignore him as a man. Just why that should bother him he didn't want to analyze. Prodding her into acknowledging his existence had the effect of simply reinforcing her professional demeanor. The end result generated in him an overwhelming desire to yank her against his chest and kiss her into submission.

The vivid image that exploded inside his head brought him up short.

"How's she doing?" Mark asked the question more to stop his outrageous thoughts than for the answer. He could see for himself that Beth was much better. She dozed in Catherine's arms as if sitting in a virtual stranger's lap on the way to the hospital was a routine occurrence in her life. In actuality Beth seldom allowed anyone closer than arm's length. Certainly not her father, he acknowledged grimly.

Catherine answered by rote. "As well as can be expected."

"Why do you do that?" he asked evenly.

"Do what?" Catherine countered. She was too tired

to play guessing games, though on some level she recognized that she was probably playing one herself.

"Use that damned businesslike tone. Is it some kind of ego trip for you?" He knew that wasn't the case. But he wanted to provoke a response—a genuine response—from her.

Lord, the man was exasperating. "Look, Mr. Garrett—"

"Is it me, or do you treat anyone who isn't a patient this way?" He asked the question almost as if her answer didn't really matter.

Some underlying note warned that she was wiser not to respond.

"No, that can't be right," he continued almost pleasantly. "As I remember it, you carried on a very friendly chat with the captain on the plane. Definitely less than strictly professional." The last word was flavored with distaste. "I guess I just answered my own question, huh?"

Professional. Her weary brain latched onto the word. She'd be fine if she remained professional. Like a litany, she silently chanted it. Except she didn't feel fine. She felt shaky. And scared. Not scared as in fear of physical harm. But scared as in fear of something potentially much more devastating.

Catherine's gaze dueled with his before he returned his attention to the road. "That's what I am—a professional. And that's the capacity in which I am dealing with you and Beth." She hoped she sounded in control. She *knew* she sounded priggish.

"What more do you want from me?" she goaded, astonishing herself. She was deliberately trying to provoke him!

Catherine watched his expression take on a sensual twist, starting with his hard mouth then moving up into his eyes. Without her guessing his intent, he reached over and ran a bold finger ever so gently down her left cheek.

"Now there's a question." Mark observed with interest the anger ignite in her. There was passion in her. Hidden deep, and tightly leashed. He doubted she was even aware of it. But he could sense it. And he wanted to experience it.

"It would be my . . . pleasure to show you." His voice was Kentucky-bourbon smooth, the provocative words running over her like invisible hands.

Catherine jerked her head away from the seductive touch as if she'd been burned. The illicit sensations this man stirred in the lower regions of her stomach were alarming. Aware of Mark's silent chuckle, she decided to withdraw and regroup and prudently clamped down on her tongue.

Laughing quietly at her refusal to respond to his subtle taunt, Mark let his hand drop back to the seat between them.

The remainder of the short trip to the hospital was accomplished in silence. When they arrived at St. Croix General, Catherine was immeasurably relieved to find Steve impatiently awaiting them in Emergency, not only because she felt too tired to be medically proficient, but also because she needed to put some distance between herself and Mark Garrett.

After taking one look at Catherine's weary expression, Steve took over. He instructed that Beth be taken to an examining room for preliminary evaluation by hospital staff, then turned his attention to Catherine, enfolding her in a fierce bear hug.

All the while a nurse harassed Mark with admissions paperwork, neither the subsequent friendly exchange nor the masculine arm that remained draped over Catherine's shoulder escaped his notice. Nor the ease with which Catherine talked with the man. *She sure doesn't have any trouble dealing with this guy in a nonprofessional manner.*

Suddenly aware of Mark Garrett's narrowed eyes on her, Catherine hastily extricated herself from Steve's hold, trying to quell the vague feeling of guilt assailing her. Grabbing Steve's arm, she said, "Come on, I want you to meet someone."

"You mean the guy who's been visually slicing me into very small pieces for the last ten minutes?" Steve asked innocently.

Catherine directed a speaking look at her friend and headed toward Mark Garrett.

As they approached, Mark's eyes flicked from Catherine to the man whose arm she clutched.

"Mr. Garrett, I'd like you to meet Dr. Steve Dalton," she began stiltedly. "He's head of staff, an excellent doctor, and a very dear friend." She couldn't imagine why she'd tacked on that last bit of information and mentally berated herself.

And just how do we define "dear"? Mark silently queried.

"Steve, this is Mark Garrett, Beth's father."

Each man took the other's measure, Steve extending his hand first. Mark hesitated a fraction of a second before clasping it. He registered the firm grip, the direct eye contact, and conceded that under different circumstances he'd probably have liked the guy.

"Dalton."

Steve overlooked the terse acknowledgment. "Glad to meet you, Mr. Garrett." He had difficulty concealing a smile. "They'll be taking Beth up to Radiology shortly. You can see her as soon as they're finished with the preliminary lab work.''

"Dr. Chambers will be taking care of Beth," Mark stated unequivocally.

"No problem." Steve's words of assurance were congenial. "We'll be delighted to have CJ on staff here in any capacity. We've been trying to get her here on a permanent basis."

Catherine opted for escape. "I'm going to check on Beth. I promised her I wouldn't be long. Mr. Garrett, Steve will be happy to answer any questions you might have. If you'll excuse me?''

"Go on. I'm certain Mr. Garrett and I will find something to talk about for the next few minutes. Oh, and CJ?'' Steve called after her as she headed toward the cubicle where Beth waited, "I'm ready to go home whenever you are.''

"Right," she answered with a wave. Not looking back, she missed the cynical condemnation in gray eyes the exact shade of gun metal.

The examination area where Beth waited was small and cluttered with medical equipment. "Hi, honey," Catherine said, walking over to the girl. "Are they taking good care of you?''

Beth's slight nod revealed her uneasiness at whatever was to happen next.

"You're going up to X-ray now, so put on a happy face." She playfully tapped Beth's nose. "They're going to take some pictures of you.''

Mark entered the cubicle in time to hear Beth ask anxiously, "Will you come with me?''

"You bet," Catherine assured her.

He watched the apprehension recede from Beth's face

and was again grateful to this woman for her soothing influence on his daughter.

"Can Daddy come, too?"

Mark had difficulty concealing his surprise at his daughter's impulsive request. This was the first time he could remember Beth asking for him. Maybe there was a chance to strengthen the tenuous bond between them before . . .

Catherine glanced up and, for an unguarded moment, smiled warmly at him. The transformation in her serene features took his breath away, scattering his bleak thoughts.

"Well, he can't go where they'll take the x-rays." Beth's disappointment was genuine, and Catherine quickly added, "But I'll bet he'll be waiting for you when you get out. Will that be okay?"

Mark hadn't anticipated his daughter's look of intense relief. Knowing Beth needed him, and that this woman was somehow responsible for her expressing that need, did strange things to him. He had an overpowering urge to reach out to Catherine. Instead, he thrust his hands deep into his pockets. He didn't want to see her withdraw from him again.

Mark negligently propped one shoulder against the wall, his eyes tracking Catherine's progress up and down the hospital corridor outside Beth's room. Having been assured to his satisfaction that his daughter was going to be all right, Mark could focus his attention on Catherine. Her right hand was worrying at what he was certain were very tense muscles in her slender neck as she paced the hall in a valiant effort to ignore him.

"I have to hand it to you, Doctor. You do have a way with kids." Irony tinged his words. The easy rapport between Beth and Catherine churned conflicting emotions within him. On the one hand, he was relieved to see Beth opening up to someone—God knew, she rarely did. On the other, he couldn't stifle the vague sense of betrayal that it was to this woman rather than him.

Catherine stopped pacing and allowed her hand to drop to her side. She slowly opened her eyes to find him studying her and couldn't shake the feeling that he perceived far more than she would like. His smile, such as it was, didn't quite reach his eyes. "Thank you. I think."

"I'm sorry." He sighed. He hated apologies. "Really, I appreciate all you've done for Beth. This whole ordeal could've been so much worse if not for you." Almost as an afterthought he added, "I sure couldn't supply what she needed."

His self-derision troubled her. "There's no right or wrong way to do it, Mr. Garrett. Simply being there is what's important. Beth obviously cares a great deal for you, and you certainly helped comfort her. Children are very resilient, particularly at her age." She could detect the turmoil underlying his composed features. "Beth's very likable and easy to work with. You're very fortunate to have her."

"You don't know the half of it."

Something in his tone warned Catherine that pursuing the subject further might not be wise. "Forgive me again, Mr. Garrett. I seem to keep blundering into areas that aren't my business. Too few hours of sleep in the last forty-eight, I'm afraid."

Before she could retreat completely behind her facade, Mark pointed out mildly, "You know, you can't ignore me forever." She'd managed at some point to put her escaping hair back up into a rather haphazard chignon. He speculated briefly just how long it was and how it would look draped over her bare back and shoulders.

Catherine felt the familiar sizzle of excitement curling through her system. "I'm not ignoring you," she said more sharply than intended, wanting to pretend she didn't understand what he meant. But her innate sense of honesty surfaced. "No. You're right, I am."

Lazy interest sharpened into alert scrutiny. His body tensed, and he waited for her to continue, his gaze steady on her down-turned head.

She concentrated on the shiny black-and-white tiles at her feet and sighed, then raised her eyes to meet his almost defiantly. His pose remained deceptively casual, but she detected the controlled expectancy in him. "You're a very disturbing man, Mr. Garrett."

Mark pushed away from the wall and strolled toward her. "And how," he asked, his voice velvety, "do I disturb you?"

With difficulty Catherine contained the inclination to flee, ordering herself to hold her ground. Her eyes locked with his in wary anticipation. He came to a stop scant inches from her. Lifting his hand, he laid one finger in a feather-light caress on the rapid pulse beat at the base of her throat.

He watched her eyes dilate at his touch. They were the color of warm whiskey, rimmed in charcoal. A man could get drunk, he decided, just looking into them. Her complexion was flawless, requiring not even the hint of discreetly applied makeup she wore.

Mark felt her tremble and wondered if it was due to his touch or because she was so near exhaustion. He wanted to believe it was the former, but he was learning not to jump to conclusions regarding this woman.

The immediate lurch of her heart didn't surprise Catherine, but she did find it distressing. She should be getting used to it—this unruly rampage of her senses each time she encountered this man at close range. Even on the plane, at the height of the chaos, she hadn't been immune to him. Now, with the crisis over, there was no buffer to his magnetism. Catherine forced herself to break the contact and moved a few feet away.

"Catherine?" It was the first time he'd called her anything other than Dr. Chambers—and always tinged with mockery.

Her composure slipped another notch. She felt awkward—like a schoolgirl on her first date instead of a thirty-five-year-old experienced woman. And that was the problem, she thought. She might be experienced, but those experiences had been traumatic. "CJ," Catherine corrected a little too quickly. "My name is CJ."

Mark followed her and stopped again within touching distance, not too close but close enough to keep her from bolting.

"No." He caught an escaped tendril of her hair, testing its mahogany silkiness with his fingers. "Not CJ." One side of his sculptured mouth lifted slightly. "CJ has a cold, masculine sound to it." His hungry gaze drifted over her face, coming to rest on full lips bare of artificial coloring. "We both know you're neither." His head dipped and his voice grew huskier. "And you're much too regal for Cathy or Cat. Yes, definitely Catherine."

Catherine—not CJ. It sounded so . . . intimate when he said it. An involuntary tremor shook her, and she tried to fortify herself against his sensual invasion.

His eyes returned to hers to investigate the gold flecks that flared in their depths. "You're not married?" He already knew the answer. He'd learned that much from Dalton.

Spellbound, she shook her head mutely.

"Living with someone?" Dalton hadn't been as forthcoming with this bit of information.

Catherine was mesmerized by his seductive voice and increasingly intimate questions. She wasn't sure what compelled her, but she couldn't seem to stop herself from answering. Again she gave a negative shake.

Mark leaned closer, his body almost brushing hers, his voice dropping to a gritty whisper. "Sleeping with someone?"

Held captive by his provocative words, she allowed her eyes to explore his face. He was so close she could clearly see the inch-long jagged scar etched deeply into his left check. The old laceration had been clumsily sutured, she noted absently. Her fingers ached to trace its irregular design and imprint it on her memory. It was mute evidence of more than his share of life's harsher experiences. As she was about to raise her hand, he ran a finger over her lower lip with exquisite care, reminding her that he was waiting for an answer.

"Dalton, maybe?" he prompted.

His insolence broke the sensual spell, and Catherine's usually well-controlled temper came to her rescue. "Do you consider that any of *your* business?" She tried to pull away, but his large body blocked her retreat.

Her display of indignation seemed to amuse him. He definitely didn't appear the least remorseful for his audacity. Nor did he allow her to step away from him. "I'll tell you why I disturb you," he whispered, focusing on her mouth.

Bad mistake, Catherine chastised herself. She should never have admitted that. Her eyes touched on the scar again. It fit. Far from detracting from his looks, it added to the dangerously alluring quality about him. She knew better than to give any man, most particularly *this* man, an opening. "Forget I said—"

"You want me. You'd like to deny it. But you won't."

His blunt statement sent a tingle of renewed excitement dancing along her spine. Was she that transparent? she wondered a little desperately.

"But don't let it bother you, baby." His voice was intense, his gaze hot. "I can promise you I'm with you every step of the way."

Catherine couldn't seem to get enough air into her lungs.

How long the nurse had been standing there expectantly, Catherine couldn't have said. It was only when she heard "You can come say good night now. Beth's settled and waiting for you" that her presence finally penetrated.

Catherine inhaled sharply. "Thank you." Her voice wasn't quite steady and the small display of uncertainty seemed to please Mark. This time when she stepped around him, he let her go.

Beth smiled sleepily at Catherine as she walked over to the bed. When his daughter reached for his hand, Mark's heart squeezed inside his chest at the small, affectionate act.

Leaning over the bed railing, Catherine brushed the hair away from Beth's forehead, her hand not quite steady. After examining the purpling contusion again, she said, "Get a good night's sleep, and by tomorrow you'll feel much better."

"You'll come and see me in the morning, won't you?" Beth questioned.

Catherine waited a beat.

"You promised you'd take care of me. You haven't forgotten, have you?" Serious gray eyes, a softer version of the father's, did not waver from Catherine's troubled brown ones.

Somewhere in the back of Catherine's mind she recognized that some invisible trap had sprung shut. She closed her eyes briefly, then refocused on Beth. "No, I haven't forgotten. Go to sleep now, you need to rest. I'll see you tomorrow."

As Catherine turned to leave, Beth caught her hand. "Will you kiss me good night, please?"

An almost imperceptible movement of the man standing only inches away drew Catherine's gaze to his face. Her breath caught at the longing etched there before it was obliterated by resignation. Quickly she leaned down and placed a soft kiss on Beth's cheek, receiving one in return. "Good night, honey. I'll see you in the morning."

"Night." Reassured, Beth was asleep within minutes, and Catherine was out of the room mere seconds thereafter.

In the hallway Mark caught her arm, swinging her around to face him. Deliberately placing his right hand in the middle of her chest, he backed Catherine against the wall. His fingers lay squarely between her breasts, touching neither but tantalizing both, heating much more than just the area where his hand rested. "Don't disappoint her. She's had enough of that in her life." His voice was low with a ruthless undertone. "If you plan to disappear, tell her. Don't leave her hanging, and don't lie to her."

Catherine bristled at the flagrant insult even as she wondered what had precipitated it. "I don't lie, Mr. Garrett. And I don't abandon my patients."

He regarded her enigmatically for several long seconds before saying, "Maybe not, but I've learned from experience that the female of the species isn't known for keeping her word."

"That's the second time you've insulted my integrity, Mr. Garrett. I'd appreciate it if you'd refrain from doing so in the future."

Knocking his hand away, she hissed, "Now if you'll excuse me, I need to get some rest."

"So," Steve demanded cheerfully an hour or so later, "tell me about your Mark Garrett." It was late, well past midnight, and Catherine was sitting on the patio of Steve's villa, overlooking the small town of Christiansted.

"He's not 'my' anything." Catherine bolted from the lounge chair she'd been relaxing on only moments before and began to pace the patio deck. "What's there to tell? He's crude, egotistical, presumptuous, and, among other things, a pain in the—"

Laughing softly, Steve threw up his hands in a sign of surrender. "Okay, okay. Calm down. I just wanted to know more about this guy who can get a rise out of you."

Catherine shot him a withering look. Stopping at the concrete railing, she surveyed the twinkling lights of the harbor town below, gathering her thoughts. Turning back to face Steve, she leaned against the cool cement. "There really isn't much to tell. I met him on the plane because of the emergency. If his daughter hadn't been injured, we'd never have spoken."

"Don't bet on it. You may not have spoken to him, but I can guarantee he would've spoken to you," Steve assured her, humor still lurking in his eyes. "The man's interested in you. And he appears to be the type who gets what he wants. *Want* being the operative word."

"You noticed," Catherine muttered, experiencing a

sensual stirring deep inside. "Well, he certainly seems to bring out the worst in me."

"That's good. Getting riled can be very stimulating," Steve teased, coming up beside her to squeeze her in a congenial hug.

"Thanks heaps, friend," she said with false sarcasm, then pulled away and started pacing again.

"Hey, I'm just trying to be helpful here. You're the one who told me you felt something was missing in your life," he challenged gently. "Wasn't it you who called me less than a month ago, begging a place to stay while you sorted things out?"

"All right, yes, I did. But I don't think I mentioned anything about men. Particularly this one. He's a bit too overpowering for me." Her hands gestured in the night air, illustrating her agitation. "And he threatens me." When she noticed the scowl forming on Steve's face, she quickly amended, "Oh, not in a physical sense. It's more elemental than that. Almost as if he could . . . absorb me if I'd let him."

"There's nothing wrong with a little absorption—particularly if it's the right kind." Steve wiggled his eyebrows in mock lasciviousness.

Catherine chuckled in spite of herself at his attempt to lift her spirits, then sobered. "You know I won't risk my independence." Conviction underscored her words. She'd worked too long and hard for her emotional emancipation to allow anyone to threaten it.

"Now be honest, CJ, it's more than your independence you're worried about. You're attracted to him, too." When she didn't respond, he gently prodded. "Right?"

Nodding reluctantly, she quipped, "And here I thought I was immune." The effect Mark Garrett had on her was alarming. Joking about it might make it seem less threatening, but in a distant corner of her mind where she struggled to keep it locked, she again experienced the impact he'd had on her the minute their eyes first connected, recalled her body's sensual response to his arrogant questions about her personal life, remembered much too vividly the imprint of his strong hand between her breasts as he'd warned her not to disappoint his daughter.

"You haven't lived in a vacuum that long," Steve kidded her. "What's wrong with giving yourself a chance at a relationship? Even if it's only based on good old-fashioned hormones."

Steve draped his arm companionably around her, and Catherine leaned her head against his shoulder. But it wasn't that simple, she reflected. Intuition told her that Mark Garrett had the potential to hurt her—badly. Anyway, she didn't want a man in her life. She knew where that led. "My track record with relationships leaves a lot to be desired."

"That was years ago. So you made a mistake and married a jerk. That doesn't mean you have to swear off men forever, does it?" Steve's tone was gently exasperated.

"I'm not so sure *I* wasn't the jerk. If I'd been smart, I wouldn't have fallen for the first male who showed an interest in me." The traumatic end of her brief marriage, coming on the heels of a bleak childhood, had instilled a fearful appreciation for the price of emotional involvement. She had grave doubts the risk was worth it.

"Believe me, if abstinence equals intelligence, then you must be right up there with Einstein." Steve's tone was approaching irritation. "There's nothing dumb or foolish about trying to find happiness."

She stepped away from him. "Well, I certainly missed the boat in that respect."

"If you'll pardon the expression, you're older and wiser now." Steve ducked as Catherine threw him a playful punch, then continued his lecture. "It's past time you got on with life, CJ. And I mean something besides surgery."

"Exactly what are you suggesting I do?" Catherine asked, mildly annoyed. They had become friends in med school, and she loved Steve like a brother. He'd been there to help her pick up the pieces after Greg's desertion. She gave him wide latitude to probe subjects no one else would dare. But sometimes he could be downright aggravating when he became paternalistic— like now.

"Nothing drastic, for crissake." Steve reached over and gave her a gentle shake. "Get out and have some fun. Date. It doesn't have to be serious. But if this Garrett fellow lights your fire, see how much heat you can generate. What've you got to lose?"

"Such a genteel way of putting it," she remarked drily. He did, she silently conceded, have a point. She'd believed her marriage based on love, and the disillusionment at finding otherwise had been devastating. But what would happen if she knew right from the beginning that a relationship was based on simple desire, with no promises and no other expectations? Catherine pondered the idea for a few minutes, then decided she wasn't ready to pursue this too closely just yet. Instead, she hugged Steve hard. "Thanks for understanding. And for caring."

"Well, are you going to continue treating Beth?"

Catherine thought about it a minute, her eyes softening. She was getting far too attached to Beth. When the specialist had confirmed her own preliminary diagnosis that she was not seriously injured, Catherine's sense of overwhelming relief had left her shaken. The little girl was sweet, talented, and bright, and her tentative relationship with her father tugged at Catherine's heart. But Beth was a bittersweet reminder of the child she'd never had a chance to know.

Self-preservation told Catherine she should limit her contact with those two.

"I'll examine her tomorrow. If she's had an uneventful night, I'll recommend she be discharged from the hospital. Then it will be a moot point."

Feeling in control again, she said, "I think I'll turn in now. It's been a long day." She headed for the wide door leading into the villa. "See you in the morning." For her next encounter with Mark Garrett she intended to be well rested with her defenses firmly in place.

"Good night," Steve replied. "Uh, CJ?"

Catherine halted her departure and turned back to face him. "Yes?"

"Don't bet on Mark Garrett thinking it's a moot point."

Before Catherine could challenge his rejoinder, Steve slipped into the house, leaving her standing in the fragrant night air staring after his retreating back.

THREE

The first tentative rays of sunlight pushing their way through the Venetian blinds reminded Mark that he'd passed the night with little sleep. He rubbed his right hand over his face and grimaced at the scrape of day-old stubble.

"Do you think she'll come?"

Mark diverted his attention from the window view of the hospital parking lot to look at his daughter. He'd been wondering the same thing himself. After acting like a macho jerk last night, insulting the woman and then intimidating her, he didn't hold out too much hope. "I don't know, punkin. All we can do is wait and see."

Her bed angled at forty-five degrees and pillows propped behind her, Beth was carefully working on a picture. Mark was gratified that the bruise on her forehead looked less angry this morning and she was bright and alert. That somehow made it easier to ignore her preoccupation with drawing.

"CJ's nice. I like her." She glanced at her father. "You like her, too, don't you, Daddy?"

Beth could be unnervingly perceptive at times. "Yeah, I like her."

"I hope she'll come visit every day. Could we ask her to go to the beach with us when I get out of the hospital?"

The question caught Mark off guard. On his sporadic visits with his daughter, he usually had to coax her into merely leaving the house with him. She'd accompanied him on this trip with only halfhearted acquiescence. He winced remembering the ensuing bitter argument with her grandmother when he'd overridden the woman's vigorous objections. Yet just now Beth had automatically included him in her impulsive beach plans.

"I don't know, sweetheart," he hedged, hating to dampen this rare enthusiasm but having a good idea what Catherine's response to the invitation would be. "She's a busy doctor. I imagine she has a lot of things to do. She might not have time to go with us."

Beth concentrated on her drawing for several moments longer before saying quietly, "I bet if you asked her she would."

His daughter's uncharacteristic faith in him stunned Mark. Dr. Chambers was unwittingly having a beneficial effect on his precarious relationship with Beth. The shaky bond between them was the reason he'd insisted on bringing her to St. Croix. If he had a prayer in hell of success in the upcoming custody fight, he had to at least have Beth on his side.

Beth looked at him expectantly.

"I'll give it my best shot, princess." How disillusioned would his daughter be, he brooded, if he couldn't deliver?

Catherine stepped into Beth's room and practically collided with Mark Garrett. Two strong hands reached out to steady her.

"Well, good morning, Dr. Chambers."

At his mocking welcome her gaze bounced to his, and for a moment she thought she glimpsed a shadow of surprise. She instantly dismissed his look of relief, certain she'd imagined it.

He looked gloriously unkempt and all formidable male.

"Good morning, Mr. Garrett." Pulling her gaze from him, Catherine moved to Beth's bed and grasped the side rail. The cool steel under her fingers helped take her mind off the man standing only a few feet away. "Hi, Beth. Feeling better today?"

"Hello, CJ," Beth greeted, smiling eagerly at Catherine. "Can we leave? I don't like staying here, but Daddy said we had to wait for you. I'm better now."

"Yes, I can see you are." Catherine was pleased with the young girl's animation, a definite indication that she continued to improve with no serious residual. She glanced at Mark Garrett. His smile, minus its usual sardonic twist, was so unexpected that it set up an unwelcome tingle in the lower region of her stomach.

"As you can also see, it's been difficult keeping her under control until you got here." He moved closer to Catherine, his voice dropping an octave. "I didn't think you'd come."

"I said I would."

He studied her for several ponderous moments, his face again expressionless. "Yes. You did."

She detected an indecipherable message in the simple statement before he smiled and broke the tension.

"Well, Dr. Chambers, can we get out of here?" This time when he said her name, the usual mocking tone was missing.

Catherine corraled her wandering thoughts and lowered the railing to sit on the bed beside Beth. "Let's take a look, and we'll see."

Mark was again impressed with the way she kept Beth distracted throughout the examination by maintaining the easy rapport between them. Catherine still wore her cloak of professionalism, he noted, but there was something different about her today. She seemed softer, more touchable.

A colorful clasp casually directed her hair away from her face, allowing it to cascade down her back. As she leaned forward, mahogany strands drifted across one shoulder to rest provocatively against her breast. Mark caught his breath. Well, he'd wondered how long it was. Now he knew. If draped over her naked torso, it was just long enough to erotically coil around her nipples. Jerking his eyes away, he jammed his hands into his pockets and went to look out the window.

After Beth had successfully completed the battery of simple neurological tests, Catherine pronounced her fit enough to be released from the hospital. "As long as you understand," she cautioned Beth, "that you have to take it easy for the next several days. Okay?"

"Okay," Beth smilingly agreed.

Mark suddenly realized that unless he thought of something, and fast, Catherine was going to walk out of their life in a matter of seconds. A nurse's aide bearing Beth's breakfast provided the perfect opportunity.

Grabbing Catherine's arm, he headed toward the door. "I want to talk to you," he said in a low voice. "Alone." Telling his daughter he'd be back shortly, he ushered Catherine down the hallway and into a deserted waiting room.

She started to object to his presumptuous behavior, but the determination etched on his face checked her.

Releasing her arm, he paced a few feet away and

stopped, his back to her. "I need a favor," he began tersely. His rigid posture conveyed more clearly than words his distaste in asking, as if he were used to commanding, not requesting. "I'd like you to keep seeing Beth for a while."

"Maybe I didn't make myself clear, Mr. Garrett. Beth is doing fine. She'll need only routine medical follow-up." Catherine watched the muscles ripple beneath his snug shirt as he flexed his powerful shoulders.

"That's not what I'm referring to." He raked agitated fingers through his ebony hair, then continued. "She's more at ease around you. She talks to you." Swinging around, he glared at her. "Do you have any idea how rare that is for her? No, of course you don't. Kids just naturally love you."

The sarcasm was back. So that's what got under his skin, Catherine concluded on a flash of insight. His daughter could relate to her but not to him, and he was envious. Catherine knew all too well the pain of reaching out to an unapproachable loved one. How many times had she done that in her own life?

"Look, I'm a pediatric surgeon, not a—"

"Wait," he said, stopping what he already guessed would be a polite refusal. "Hear me out."

It couldn't hurt to listen, Catherine rationalized. "All right."

Studying her a minute, he took a deep breath as a diver might just before taking the plunge into deep water. "Beth's grandmother is trying to get permanent custody of her. My lawyer tells me if I can't establish a more comfortable relationship with Beth before the hearing, there's a damned good chance the— she'll succeed." Mark paused and looked at Catherine as if gauging her reaction.

His bitterness and frustration suddenly made sense.

She now could understand what drove him. With the knowledge came an unanticipated need to comfort him, and a nebulous fear that she was stepping into quicksand. "I'm not qualified for this," she said simply. "You need someone who's trained in child psychology."

"No!" He fought to temper himself. "All I'm asking is that you spend some time with us." He released an exasperated breath. "Give Beth and me a chance to get to know each other in a relaxed atmosphere, not some clinical setting. If it doesn't work out—" he shrugged fatalistically"—that'll be it. No pressure, no more demands."

"I'm not sure I understand how I can help." Catherine felt herself weakening and had to combat a small panicky feeling.

Mark captured her gaze with his. "When you're around, Beth's not so . . . uptight with me." He laughed mirthlessly. "Do you realize she's talked more to me in the last twenty-four hours than she has in months? Mostly about you."

"I don't see—"

"Look," Mark interrupted. "What are your plans for the next several days?"

"Not much really. After yesterday, I just want to rest."

"Perfect. You say Beth needs to take it easy, so why not spend some time with us—" Mark raked a hand over his tired face and frowned, remembering how long he'd been without sleep "—starting tomorrow? Picnics, swimming, sightseeing, whatever. You won't have to lift a finger, just enjoy yourself. I'll take care of everything. I'll pick you up each morning and deliver you safely back to Dalton's each evening."

Catherine considered the invitation. Why not? she asked herself. She was experiencing an odd reluctance to leave Beth—or Beth's father. The latter thought was disquieting, but she suddenly felt daring. Besides, she'd be perfectly safe as long as Beth was with them. Wouldn't she?

"What's the risk?" he prompted at her continued hesitation. "You like Beth." His smile quirked again, a subtle reminder of his lethal magnetism. "Who knows, you might find I'm not quite as bad as you believe."

That was just the problem, she thought. He wasn't as bad—he was far worse. He was chipping away at her defenses. And she understood the potential danger should he succeed.

Casually sliding his hands into the back pockets of his jeans, Mark ambled across the room to stop within a foot of Catherine. "Besides," he added quietly, "we've got unfinished business."

The abrupt change in tactics set off alarms in Catherine.. Her heart picked up speed. "Beg pardon?"

"You don't have to beg, Catherine." His husky voice was almost a physical touch. "Whatever you want from me, just name it, it's yours."

Catherine raised her hands in a weak attempt to evade him. "This isn't a good idea." Even to her own ears the words sounded lame.

"Oh, I disagree." Mark watched her tongue nervously moisten her lower lip and ached to substitute his own. "I think it's one of my best." Removing his hands from his pockets, he placed them gently on her shoulders.

When his body eased hers against the wall, Catherine was absurdly conscious of its coolness permeating her back in sharp contrast to the heat being generated inside her. Strong fingers anchored her chin, and her entire world narrowed to probing gray eyes now buffed to pewter. She braced for the emotional onslaught an instant before his mouth closed over hers. His lips were unexpectedly soft for a mouth so uncompromisingly masculine. Almost experimentally he touched, then tasted, before delving into her inner warmth.

Shocking herself, she didn't pull away. Offered no resistance. In fact, she participated fully in the mating of their mouths. The abrasion of his day-old beard against her softer skin served to enhance, rather than detract from, the primal sensations he was stirring in her.

She thought she'd prepared herself. She was wrong. The sensual shock reverberating through her left her legs too weak to hold her. His body supported hers, keeping her upright and making her brazenly conscious of his potent arousal.

Mark groaned. She smelled so good, a light lemony fragrance with an underlying hint of spice. Just like the woman, it surrounded him, pulling him closer. It echoed her taste, elusive and addicting. She was melting all over him right here in the—

Damn, what the hell was he doing? They were standing in a hospital waiting room! With considerable effort he dragged his stampeding senses under control and forced himself to lift his mouth from hers. "Damn," Mark repeated aloud, pulling a steadying breath into his lungs.

Her drugged senses making her lids uncooperative, Catherine slowly opened her eyes. "Mr. Garrett—"

"It's time to drop the formality, Catherine." His voice conveyed wry amusement. "Seems a little pointless now, don't you think?"

"Mark," she corrected weakly, her senses still chaotic. That he seemed almost unaffected by what had just happened between them angered her. It also made her feel exposed. And vulnerable.

"This," she said more forcefully, pushing against his chest, "is why I have serious reservations about getting involved with you." She used indignation in an attempt to camouflage her roiling emotions.

Mark loosened his arms, allowing her to put a sliver of space between them. Her face was faintly flushed, her lips softly swollen from the abrasion of his. The observation did not help the ache in his groin, and frustration roughened his words. "Honey, we're already involved up to our—" He broke off. "Denying it won't change it."

He released her and ran both hands through his disheveled hair. "Regardless of what's between us, I still need your help with Beth."

Catherine was amazed she didn't slide to the floor in a puddle. If not for the wall's support she guessed she probably would.

A tiny still-functioning portion of her brain persistently nagged that she couldn't desert Beth. Catherine was certain that these two people loved each other deeply. If there was the slightest chance of helping the precarious relationship between this child and her father, she'd be unable to walk away.

Her equilibrium was slowly returning along with her resolve. "All right, I'll do this for Beth. You," she said with more vehemence, "are not part of the bargain. I don't like to be pushed, Mr. Gar— Mark, and you seem to have a propensity for it. I want your word that this—" because she didn't dare define it, she resorted instead to an agitated wave of her hand "— won't happen again."

Relief washed through him. She needed some space. Fine. No problem. He'd back off and give it to her.

And bide his time. At least she wasn't denying the explosive chemistry between them. And she was willing to help him with Beth.

"Fair enough." He'd savor each small victory as it came. "We'll set some ground rules. I'll control my urge to do . . . *this*. And you'll stick around." He waited a heartbeat. "Deal?"

Again there was a challenge in his words, Catherine was certain. But she could handle it, couldn't she? Fortifying herself with a deep breath, she whispered, "Deal."

The aviator glasses Mark wore today were so opaque they obscured his eyes. They were not, however, so impenetrable as to make Catherine oblivious to his intent scrutiny. She felt the keen edge of his gaze intimately delineating her body as he followed her up the flagstone steps of his Spanish-style villa located just outside Christiansted.

The dim light filtering into the entry hall was a cool invitation after the tropical heat of the sun. She noted that he did not remove the glasses.

"It's lovely," she said in an attempt to distract herself.

"Thanks. It needs some work." Mark closed the massive front door, shutting out the heat. "That's probably why Joe left it to me. Figured it would keep me busy and out of trouble," he added, smiling wryly.

He smoothed one hand over the teak hallway bannister, enjoying the tactile stimulation of the worn wood. "From the looks of it, he was right."

Catherine followed the sensual track of his fingers over the railing, then determinedly redirected her eyes, taking in the just-short-of-shabby interior. "Looks like it has potential. This is the first time you've been here?''

He nodded once. "Joe was going to use it as an excuse to get away more often.'' Momentary sadness touched his features before being ruthlessly obliterated. "Unfortunately, he waited too long. He died before he got the chance.''

"I'm sorry.'' Though he hid it well, Catherine still felt his anguish. "Joe was a relative?''

"By blood? No. By pure sweat and tenacity?'' Mark shrugged noncommittally.

He directed Catherine into an airy room banked on two sides by windows overlooking a sheer drop to the beach below. The ocean view afforded was a breathtaking collage of jades and turquoises, but Mark gave it scant notice, soberly considering her question. He despised talking about himself. Street life had taught him early that he might not live long if he gave away many secrets. Personal revelations to a woman could be even more deadly. He knew firsthand how a female could use the knowledge to destroy his very soul.

But he'd also learned that to get what he wanted he had to pay a price. And he wanted something from Catherine.

"He dragged my ass out of enough trouble when I was a snot-nosed, smart-mouthed kid. Does that qualify him as a relative?'' He turned to face her, capturing her gaze before removing the dark glasses with calculated ease.

Mark's disparaging description of his childhood set up an ache somewhere inside Catherine. She wanted to ask where his parents were while Joe was saving him from himself, but the hard edge to his voice stopped her. Instead, she observed softly, "He must have been very special to you.''

"You might say that." Mark could see the unasked questions in her eyes. She wanted to know about him? Okay, he'd oblige her. But he'd make her work for it. And when he was ready, he'd demand reciprocation.

"If you want information, honey, you're going to have to ask. I don't give away too much for free," he warned in a silky voice.

It was on the tip of her tongue to tell him just what he could do with his *information*, but some instinct— or maybe the flicker of . . . something in the smoky depths of his eyes—made her decide against that course. "I'll remember that," she returned coolly. "All right, Mark, we'll play it your way. While Joe was saving your . . . ass, where were your parents?"

Her response surprised him. He hadn't realized until now that he admired a woman with guts.

"My mother ran off when I was twelve or thirteen." A muscle pulsed in his jaw. "I never knew who my father was."

The stark disclosure shook Catherine, but she kept her face composed, certain this man would reject pity. "And Joe took care of you?"

A quiet laugh tinged his answer with reminiscence. "When I was about seventeen, he pulled me off some street kid in danger of being beaten to a pulp and decided—God knows why—that I was worth rehabilitating. He cleaned me up, sent me into the military for a while, then taught me how to build things instead of destroying them."

She didn't question him about the years between thirteen and seventeen. Something told her it would be too painful to hear. "So, what kind of things do you build?"

Mark's gaze remained steady. "Office complexes

mostly, in and around Atlanta. But we'll—we'd tackle anything for the right price.''

He was baiting her she was sure. Everything he said had a cryptic undertone to it. With effort she disregarded her growing exasperation and tried a different tack. ''Tell me about Beth.''

''What do you want to know?''

''For starters, why is your relationship with her so strained?''

Okay, hotshot, you asked for help. She had a right to some answers. He rolled his broad shoulders in a facsimile of a shrug before expelling a deep breath. ''We don't know each other,'' he stated flatly. ''She's spent most of her life with her grandmother Alice. My wife—ex-wife—'' bitterness stained the word ''—died shortly after she was born. I was spending twenty hours a day trying to keep my construction firm out of bankruptcy.''

His fingers splayed through his hair in agitation, and he again went to stare unseeingly out the window at the panoramic view. ''What the hell did I know about taking care of a baby?''

As explanations went it was succinct and to the point. But she could decipher his unspoken reasoning. Ill equipped to care for his infant daughter, wanting the best for her, what better answer than for him to turn her over to a doting grandmother? It had been a logical—and loving—solution. But she knew intuitively he left out far more than he revealed.

''Are you saying you haven't had any contact with Beth at all?'' Catherine couldn't bring herself to believe that was the case. She'd witnessed his love for and devotion to his daughter.

''I see her. Just . . . not often.''

Mark turned back toward Catherine, his face softening. "She was so tiny when she was first born. I was terrified to touch her." He laughed disparagingly, examining his hands. "In Alice's opinion I would've inflicted irreparable harm just by holding her. That doesn't leave a lot to do with a kid."

Catherine shuddered inwardly at the bleak words. "Why is she trying to get permanent custody?"

He hesitated imperceptibly. "She claims I'm a bad influence." With exaggerated care he replaced the dark glasses.

It was as final as a door slamming.

"Come on, let's go down to the beach. Our housekeeper has been keeping Beth entertained while she waited for you." He ushered her outside through the louvered doorway, across the small yard aflame with brilliant bougainvillea and trees burgeoning with spring foliage, to a rickety wooden stairway leading down the side of the cliff.

When Catherine hesitated at the first step, Mark took her arm, flashing her a taunting grin. "They're safe enough, at least for the moment." He ran his eyes over her body, taking in the filmy garment that didn't quite conceal the figure-revealing maillot swimsuit she wore beneath it. "You don't think I'd put your delectable body at risk, do you?"

Catherine wasn't sure she'd heard him correctly. Ignoring the sizzle of awareness permeating her, she concentrated on just getting down the stairs without breaking her neck.

"Getting them repaired might take a while, though. You'll find that everything on the island is done slowly and with . . . lingering attention." He liked watching the flustered color wash up into her face. He might have promised not to kiss her, but he'd said nothing about other forms of seduction.

* * *

The damned bathing suit was perfectly respectable.
it covered every one of Catherine's essential parts.
Completely. So why was his libido in overdrive? Mark
could answer that in one word. Legs. *Long* legs. That
went on forever. He'd never been much of a leg man,
preferring voluptuousness instead. But right now he was
vividly imagining Catherine's wrapped around him in
the throes of passion. The image was about to blow off
the top of his head.

At the moment she was cavorting across the sand in
an attempt to keep up with his daughter in a game of
Frisbee. The Frisbee abruptly landed with a plop beside
his beach towel. He shifted—with no small amount of
discomfort—retrieved it, then sent it sailing in the opposite direction before Catherine had a chance to get
too close. If he hoped to hang onto his sanity, he decided, he'd better come up with some other activity that
required more than a bathing suit. Three straight days
of this was about all he could handle.

Grabbing his drink, he took a long swallow of the
cold fruit punch, then started unloading the picnic basket for lunch. It helped only moderately to bank the
fire raging in his gut.

"That's it for me today," Catherine informed him
breathlessly a short while later, dropping onto a beach
chair next to the picnic table.

"You're good with her," Mark commented mildly,
gesturing toward the water's edge where Beth still
played. "Why don't you have children of your own?"

The painful question, coming so unexpectedly, threw
Catherine. "Don't need any," she responded quickly.
"I have a practice full of them. I get to know them,
spoil them even, then send them home."

The answer was too flippant. "I don't buy it. You

obviously love them and they love you. Just look at Beth.'' Mark studied Catherine consideringly. ''You'd make a good mother.''

She frantically searched for a means to redirect the conversation. Laughing weakly, she quipped, ''Are you saying I look maternal?''

Mark paused in his lunch preparations and slowly pivoted to face her. Nonchalantly he propped one hip against the table, folding his arms over his bare chest. ''There's nothing I'd like better than to demonstrate *exactly* how I see you.'' The hunted look suffusing her features pleased him. His plan to keep her off balance might just work. If it didn't kill him first. ''Except for Beth's presence—and my promise to you—I wouldn't hesitate.''

Catherine shifted restlessly in her chair, trying to ignore his sensual taunt.

''It's not going to work, Catherine,'' he continued conversationally, not understanding his growing need to discover all there was to know about this woman. ''You can change the subject, but I *will* get the answers to my questions—one way or another.''

It was almost a threat. She wondered a little hysterically just how he'd go about obtaining them. Memories of his sensual persuasion of only a few days ago flooded her mind. Her stomach did a little somersault. Maybe the wiser move was to simply divulge the information and skip the evasion.

''I'd love to have a child,'' she said, unaware of the yearning she'd failed to disguise. ''It just never . . . worked out.''

''But not because you haven't had the opportunity.'' Some sixth sense told him he was entering forbidden territory. He didn't heed the warning. ''Ever been married?'' he probed.

She adjusted her sunglasses, hoping she appeared composed. "Several years ago. It was quite an emotional lesson." One she intended never to forget. "I thought we were building a life together, when in reality he was furthering his career."

Though the pain of being dumped for another woman had diminished, she had no wish to expose herself again. "I learned from the experience. Now I rely only on myself. And since having a child requires a man—at least at one critical stage . . ." Her voice trailed away meaningfully. "Does that answer your questions, Mr. Garrett?"

Not by a long shot, honey, Mark told Catherine silently as he watched her bolt from the chair and head in Beth's direction—away from him.

The fact that the man was annoying as hell didn't seem to curtail her appreciation of his body, Catherine thought with self-directed scorn. She settled herself more comfortably in the beach chair, relishing the umbrella's shade. She'd managed to discreetly elude Mark Garrett for the past hour. Or was he simply allowing her to assume that? she speculated uneasily.

Mark glanced up from trying to teach Beth the fundamentals of snorkeling and caught Catherine's covert inspection. Telling his daughter to stay put, he started across the brilliant expanse of sand toward her.

His body was beautiful, Catherine reluctantly admitted. *Lord, my sunglasses are the only thing saving me from being accused of voyeurism.* His burnished skin stretched tautly over muscles sculpted, not from practiced gym workouts, but from hard physical labor. And though his bathing suit wasn't immodest, she recalled with excruciating clarity the hot imprint of what it covered and felt an answering heat concentrating between her thighs.

Hands on hips, head cocked to one side, he stopped directly in front of her, filling her entire field of vision with his blatant masculinity.

"Are you going to sulk for the rest of the day?" he asked without preamble.

She averted her eyes. "I don't sulk, Mr. Garrett."

"Right." He wanted to ask if she ran from everything unpleasant, but decided this time to heed the warning signals telling him to back off. "Come help me with Beth. She's afraid to put her face in the water. Maybe if you're there, she'll relax."

"If she doesn't want to learn, why are you insisting?" Catherine recognized on some objective level that she was being petulant.

Mark's look was censuring. "Being a doctor, you, of all people, should realize the danger in not knowing how to swim."

Growing up on the streets he'd learned that no bit of knowledge was useless. His survival had often depended upon it. In the course of his work with street kids, he passed on as much practical information as he could. He wanted nothing less for his daughter. Holding out a hand to Catherine, he waited patiently for her to take it.

Catherine felt reprimanded, and justifiably so. Reining in her indignation, she placed her hand in his and followed him.

When they reached Beth, Mark said gently, "Catherine's going to learn how to snorkel with us."

"I'd rather not just now, Daddy." Beth's voice was plaintive.

Mark hunkered down so that he was eye level with his daughter. "Punkin, if we learn about the things that scare us, they don't seem so bad anymore.'' His persuasive reasoning held unexpected compassion.

With uncertainty Beth considered his logic, then looked beseechingly at Catherine. "He's right, honey. Everyone should know how to swim.''

Still looking skeptical, Beth allowed Catherine and Mark to lead her into the crystalline water. Mark's patience seemed inexhaustible, and within a brief period Beth was eagerly practicing with her face mask and snorkel.

Catherine hadn't envisioned such a hard man possessing so much patience—and gentleness. Once past the initial awkward stage, Mark worked with Beth like a pro. Almost as if he regularly dealt with obstinate children.

When father and daughter had established an easy rapport, Catherine left them to themselves and went to sit on the warm, blinding-white sand to watch from a distance. He was making good progress with her, Catherine observed, and she felt a curious sense of satisfaction in seeing Beth relax and open up with Mark.

The comfortable camaraderie continued as all three later explored the pristine shoreline. It was only when Catherine suggested that Beth sketch the shell she was admiring that the first sign of strain reappeared. Mark didn't comment. Instead, he turned abruptly and walked away.

"Daddy doesn't like me to draw," Beth said gloomily as she watched her father's retreating back.

Catherine wondered if Mark had any idea how his seeming insensitivity to his daughter's artistic endeavors hampered their relationship. "Well, I wouldn't say that," she equivocated, pulling Beth's drawing pad from the tote she carried. "He's probably just tired right now."

"My grandmother says it's 'cause he's mean."

The matter-of-fact words stole Catherine's breath. With extreme care she asked, "Do you think she's right?"

Beth shook her head, concentrating on her drawing. "Uh-uh, but Grandmother's always telling me bad things about Daddy."

Shaken, Catherine groped for a clue as to how to proceed. "Oh?" she asked with feigned casualness. "Like what?"

Beth picked up the shell and studied it intently. "That he killed my mother." It was said very quietly.

The words slammed into Catherine with the force of a fist to her solar plexus. But not for an instant did she doubt the inaccuracy of the charge. Nor question her own absolute certainty. *Dear God!* she thought, having to struggle to retain her composure, *I'm almost afraid to ask the next question.* "Do you believe her?"

Catherine's heart ached as she watched Beth seriously deliberate her answer. "No," she finally said with conviction. "He couldn't do something that bad."

The certainty in the child's voice went a long way toward restoring Catherine's equilibrium. But she sensed the subject should not be dropped just yet. "You seem very sure," she cautiously prodded.

"Oh, I am." Beth nodded gravely. " 'Cause he helps people. 'Cept maybe for Grandmother. Sometimes they yell at each other. But he doesn't with anybody else. And even when I do something that makes him real mad, he's still nice. He just explains to me why I shouldn't do it."

Catherine suddenly became conscious of Mark standing, along with his housekeeper, only a few feet away. The pallor beneath his deep tan confirmed that he'd overheard. But the fury in his eyes defined his mood.

"Beth," he said with controlled casualness, "get your things and go up to the house with Thelma."

Beth readily complied, unaware of the heartrending havoc her innocent words had inflicted.

Mark waited until his daughter and Thelma had started up the cliff stairs before pinning Catherine with eyes that blazed with leashed violence. "Now you understand what I'm fighting."

Catherine could do little more than nod.

Mark walked a few feet away and stared out at the restless sea. She felt the impact of his pain and disbelief and knew the hurt he was experiencing firsthand must be numbing.

"I will win." Mark's voice was gratingly low, the softness alone accentuating his resolve. "I'll *never* desert any child of mine. Beth won't go through the hell of believing her father doesn't want her." He swung around to face Catherine. "And no one is going to take her away from me. Most definitely not that bitch."

His pain, though concealed now, wrapped around Catherine's heart. Unbidden came the certainty that this man would make a ruthless and unrelenting enemy. Having glimpsed his bleak past, and now discovering what Beth was contending with, Catherine knew this was one battle Mark would win no matter what the cost.

FOUR

Mark rolled restlessly onto his back, rearranging the twisted sheet across his naked hips. Times like this he wished he did drugs, or drank heavily, or at the very least still smoked—anything that would blot out the anguish caused by his daughter's too-quiet voice. *He killed my mother.* The words echoed and reechoed in his head.

He'd suspected he was up against tough odds. He just hadn't realized the extent of Alice's hostility toward him. His fury had abated to some degree, but not enough so that he could sleep. Jamming one arm behind his head, he stared up at the shadowy patterns on the ceiling.

Paul Martin had been very explicit on what he must do to win this custody fight: establish a closer relationship with Beth. Now, having learned what his daughter had been told about him, he figured that might take considerably longer than he'd first hoped. Even with Catherine's help.

But the attorney had also told him that a stable home

environment was equally important to the court. Maybe his best bet was to find a suitable mother for Beth.

Interesting idea, that, Mark mused.

Bunching a second pillow behind his back, he levered himself into a sitting position. Marriage to Elise had permanently inoculated him against the institution. He could still hear her taunting voice threatening to destroy their unborn child—until he'd found a way to stop her. She'd wanted money and her freedom in exchange for the life of his child. He'd been more than happy to give her both.

In the process, he thought ironically, he'd set himself up for the very situation he was in right now. The divorce settlement had almost wiped him out financially, and he'd had to work long hours in order to save his company. He'd had little choice but to leave Beth with Alice after Elise's death. But it had been a mistake. He hadn't realized the older woman was as vindictive as her daughter. He shifted against the distasteful memories. Once again he'd stupidly trusted a woman.

A man was a fool if he didn't learn from his mistakes.

He'd sworn never to try marriage again. Never to open himself up to the potential pain. But he'd also sworn never to desert Beth as he'd been deserted. In frustration he clenched one hand into a fist. Nor had he ever considered that someone would try to take his daughter from him.

A quick inventory of women he'd dated during the last couple of years turned up no potential candidate. He hadn't expected to find one. Superficial females tended not to be very maternal.

An image of Catherine seemed to materialize on the dimly lit wall across from him. In a figure-hugging swimsuit, with her hair in disarray, she was anything but maternal. But then came the indelible memory of Catherine quietly, delicately, talking with Beth about her grandmother's appalling accusations about him. She'd handled that with the sensitivity of someone who cared deeply. As a mother might with her daughter.

Why wasn't she involved with someone? She had to be in her early thirties at least. Not that all the off-limits signs she kept posted were conducive to attracting a man. His chest lifted on a self-mocking chuckle. Those same warnings sure hadn't seemed to discourage *him*.

The more he learned about Catherine, the more she intrigued him. Her brief, stark explanation about her childlessness and her marriage served only to make him more determined to uncover all she'd left out. Her haunting pain, carefully disguised in anger, had disturbed him more than he cared to admit.

Vulnerable. He didn't like dealing with a vulnerable woman. A man could too easily hurt her unintentionally. He felt compelled to discover the cause of her pain. And he could expose his own weaknesses in the process.

In fact, he reflected sardonically, there were damned few things about Catherine that *should* attract him. Exasperated, he threw the sheet aside. His brain might understand this logic, but his body didn't seem to be listening.

All he had to do was look at her perfectly shaped mouth to recall with scalding clarity that one kiss—and her reaction to it. Groaning, he stroked his hand down his bare torso and raised one knee to ease the swelling heaviness in his groin.

A breeze ruffled the gauzy curtains but did little to cool his heated body. One way or the other he was

going to have her. That, or he was going to go quietly
out of his mind.

But first he was going to get some answers.

He angled his head to look at the clock on the
nightstand. One forty-seven A.M. He wasn't supposed
to pick up Catherine until two-thirty tomorrow. Correc-
tion, *today*.

It was going to be a long twelve-plus hours.

But it wasn't Catherine who opened the door the next
afternoon.

"Mr. Garrett." Steve Dalton seemed congenial enough
on the surface, but there was an underlying hint of
steel.

"The name's Mark." Mark studied the man standing
in the shadowed hallway. His eyes conveyed a reservation that told Mark he was in for more than polite
pleasantries.

"All right. Mark. Come in." Steve moved aside,
allowing him to enter. "CJ's still out running errands."

"Thanks." Mark glanced at his watch as he stepped
into the cool interior. "Think she'll be long?" He realized he was way too early, but he'd awakened with an
urgent need to see Catherine.

"You're very intent on monopolizing a great deal of
CJ's time," Steve casually observed.

The proprietary remark grated. "You have a prior
claim on her time?"

Steve's expression remained bland as he ushered
Mark into a large, open living room which led directly
onto a patio beyond. "My only claim on CJ is one of
friendship and concern. Care for a drink?"

Mark ignored the invitation. "Is there a point here,
Dalton?"

Steve eyed him consideringly, before walking over

to the bar. "I haven't quite made up my mind about you, Mark."

"I didn't realize I was on trial," Mark commented drily.

Disregarding the sarcasm, he continued. "You could be the best thing that ever happened to CJ. Or the worst."

"She's a big girl. She can decide that for herself."

"Yes, I suppose she can. I simply want to ensure that she decides before she's hurt."

Mark's eyes turned icy and his voice grew dangerously quiet. "What makes you think I would hurt her?"

"Because you don't know anything about CJ."

"Since I'm spending so much time with Catherine," Mark drawled, the accompanying smile lacking even a trace of warmth, "I imagine I'll learn what I need to know."

"That's my point. You won't. Or at least it won't be easy. CJ doesn't talk much about herself."

"Don't underestimate my determination," Mark advised.

Steve assessed Mark's expressionless face. "I'm going to take a chance on you, Mark Garrett. I hope I don't regret it." He picked up a decanter from the bar and again queried, "Drink?"

This time Mark didn't decline. "Whiskey. Straight." He needed it to calm the seething anger igniting in him. The relationship between Catherine and this guy bugged him. And he resented the fact that Steve Dalton apparently believed Catherine needed protection from him. With difficulty he hung onto his temper and braced for the inevitable lecture.

"CJ had a bastard for a father and an even bigger one for a husband," he related baldy, watching Mark closely.

The declaration was not what he'd expected. "I'm

listening.'' Though Mark uttered the words off-handedly, Dalton now had his full attention.

Steve walked over and handed Mark his drink. "She had a miserable childhood. Until his death, her father kept Catherine jumping through hoops trying to please him.'' Steve shook his head sadly. "In his eyes she never measured up to his formidable expectations, and he made sure she knew it.''

"Her mother?'' Mark questioned.

"Ah, yes, her mother. She ran off when CJ was a child.''

The similarity between his and Catherine's childhood left a curious ache inside Mark. He waited for Steve Dalton to continue.

"As for her husband—well, let's just say he was a jerk who used CJ for his own selfish purposes and leave it at that.'' Steve looked speculatively at Mark. "Understandably, she's developed a healthy mistrust of men.''

Mark downed a large swallow of the liquor and welcomed its fiery heat. He wasn't sure if the fury gripping him now was directed at Dalton for questioning his intentions or at the faceless bastards who'd hurt Catherine. When the other man added nothing further, Mark muttered tightly, "I gather this is all the information you're offering.''

"Correct. If CJ wants you to know the particulars, she'll have to tell you. The point is, she generally steers clear of men.''

"With the exception of you.''

"With the exception of me.''

Mark's eyes narrowed at the confirmation.

"I'm telling you this now,'' Dalton continued, "because CJ's very vulnerable at the moment.''

Vulnerable. Yeah, he knew. "What's the bottom line here, Dalton?"

"Usually she guards herself scrupulously against personal entanglements. You seem to have touched a cord in her that few ever reach. See that you don't hurt her."

A rigid knot formed in Mark's jaw. "Will it put your mind at rest," he asked, his voice tight, "if I give you my word that the very last thing I want to do with Catherine is hurt her?"

"There are ways of hurting and ways of hurting," he replied.

Mark would have liked to pursue that cryptic remark, but the sound of a car in the driveway interrupted.

Not flinching under Mark's cold gray stare, Steve said, "That should be CJ now."

Before opening the door to admit her, he turned to Mark and suggested complacently, "Incidentally, please call me Steve."

Mark looked haggard, Catherine decided once Steve had left them alone. His face showed signs of a restless night, but none of the fury and pain she'd witnessed briefly yesterday. His steady regard was making her unusually self-conscious. Normally she had no trouble ignoring a man's sexual appraisal.

Of course, that was before Mark Garrett.

"Hope I didn't keep you waiting long. I was looking for something for Beth," she related in an attempt to fill the conversational void.

Mark remained silent, his disturbing gaze unwavering. Bracing herself, she finally asked, "Do you want to talk about it?"

He didn't pretend to misunderstand. "I don't need you to wipe my nose, Catherine."

His sarcasm hurt more than she'd anticipated. "And I wasn't offering pity."

"No?" Heat stirred in him as his eyes traveled the length of her. Well, he'd succeeded in getting her into something other than a bathing suit. But the silky green jumpsuit, though hiding more than it revealed, accentuated her newly acquired tan and emphasized the length of her legs—and did nothing to appease his hunger.

His gaze returned to her face. Today she'd woven her hair into a French braid even more enticing than the carefree style she'd worn on the beach. The effect aroused in him a desire to sink his hands into it and ravage its prim symmetry. She looked luscious. And, he thought in frustration, she was totally unaware of the erotic effect she was having on him.

"Would you like me to tell you what I *do* need from you?"

Catherine steadied her voice with difficulty caused as much by irritation as by his suggestive words. "That's right. I'm supposed to ask *specific* questions if I want information."

Mark sighed and raked a hand through his hair. "Sorry. I shouldn't take out my frustration on you." He'd done more apologizing to this woman than to anyone in memory. "To answer your question—no, I don't want to talk about it. But I don't imagine I'll have a choice."

"We don't have to discuss anything you don't want to."

An unexpected look of relief crossed his face, immediately replaced by a provocative smile. Casually he walked over to Catherine, halting within inches of her, and smoothed the back of one index finger over her flushed cheek. The act was so natural she didn't think to pull away. "Good. I can think of much more . . .

pleasant things to do than talk." The smile became a sensual grin.

"Don't look so hunted, Catherine," he chided gently. "I was merely referring to spending the afternoon with you and Beth."

His touch sparked the now-familiar frisson of excitement, along with the urge to bolster her defenses. "Give me a minute to get Beth's gift, and we can leave."

Mark's forehead furrowed quizzically. "Gift?"

"Yes. I thought it would be nice if she experimented with pastels. She really is talented."

The furrows deepened into disapproval.

Again his reaction baffled Catherine. "Mark, I don't understand this hangup you have with Beth's artwork. You'd think she was asking for permission to use a controlled substance or something equally repulsive."

All traces of his earlier smile were obliterated. "Believe me, it can be almost that bad," Mark informed her curtly. "Okay, you want the story? I'll give it to you."

He went to the bar and refilled his glass. "My mother thought she was an artist." Scorn underscored his words. "In fact, her life was devoted to pursuing art. Nothing and no one interfered with it—certainly not her son."

The bitter facts sliced into Catherine, along with a powerful need to comfort him. "Was she talented?" she asked, in a vain search for some neutral ground.

His expletive was crude and to the point. "I don't know nor care. What I do know is that I watched art become an obsession—a sickness—with her. One day I came home—" he braced himself against the edge of the bar "—and she was gone. No note. Nothing. I learned from a neighbor that she'd joined some artists' commune. She was going to pursue her career. I never heard from her again.''

The eyes that imprisoned Catherine's were as cold as slate. ''I will not see that happen to Beth.'' His inner turmoil barely contained, he left his untouched drink on the bar and strode through the open doorway onto the patio.

The details of his mother's desertion were as painful as she'd feared. Following him a few moments later, she offered no words of sympathy, knowing they would be misconstrued as pity. Impulsively she laid her hand hesitantly on his broad back, absorbing the feel of rigid muscles bunched beneath the thin material of his shirt. The contact was electric.

Curling her hand against the shock, she pointed out with gentle logic, ''Beth is *not* your mother.''

Mark's head snapped up at her touch, but he kept his back to her, staring unseeingly at the myriad of colorful sailing craft bobbing in the harbor below. ''This is none of your business,'' he warned in a flat voice.

She took a deep breath to ease the ache of his rejection. ''You made it my business, Mark,'' Catherine reminded him quietly. ''Every time you show your disapproval of Beth's work, you add to the strain in your relationship. She's a dear, sweet child who wants very much to please you. Art is the only really constant thing in Beth's life. It's her way of showing love. Don't you see? You can't take that away from her. It would be like denying a part of Beth.''

He was silent for so long she was afraid he considered the subject closed. Finally, still not facing her, he asked gruffly, ''You really believe that? That she could be encouraged to draw and not become obsessed by it?'' The disbelief remained.

Restraining the compassion in her voice wasn't easy. "You don't have a choice, Mark. You have to give her the option to do what she loves."

It was almost like admitting defeat, Mark thought in derision. But he was out of his depth and knew it. Give him a grown woman and he had a clue of how to relate to her. But his seven-year-old daughter? No, he had no choice. He'd have to take a chance on Catherine's advice. Turning to face her, he lifted his hands in resignation. "Okay. Assuming you're right, what should I do? How do I handle this?"

It was the first time Catherine had witnessed uncertainty in Mark, and she found it strangely endearing. "Try controlling your disapproval. Occasionally compliment her on her work. Not, for heaven's sake, by gushing over everything she does," she added lightly, attempting to relieve some of the tension. "Simply let her know that her attempts at art have merit. Then tell her she can begin art lessons when you get back to Atlanta."

At her last suggestion his dubious look returned.

"What's the worst that could happen?" Catherine continued quickly before he could voice his dissent. "If she starts neglecting other areas of her life, you can always stop the lessons. But if she doesn't, you've demonstrated your trust in her and your understanding of how important this is to her." In unconscious appeal she placed one hand on his chest. "Either way you can't lose."

He assessed the earnestness on Catherine's features. He'd never considered it from Beth's point of view. He ran both hands down his face and released a heavy sigh. "Get your things and let's go pick up Beth. Maybe if I work at it, I'll come up with a graceful way to do an about-face."

* * *

"CJ, come and look," Beth called as Mark ushered Catherine into the villa several days later.

In the living room painted golden with afternoon sunlight, Beth was leaning over a stroller containing a very small baby. From the color-coordinated clothing and accessories, Catherine surmised the infant was a girl. She sucked in a fortifying breath. Though she worked daily with children in her practice, she still felt a bittersweet pang at the sight of a newborn.

As if sensing her subtle distress, Mark took her arm as they mounted the shallow stairs leading into the room. Though the gesture could be considered nothing more than common courtesy, somehow it supplied the modicum of reassurance Catherine needed.

"Isn't she adorable?" Beth crooned. "Her name's Michelle, and she's just six weeks old. Thelma's her grandmother, and she's letting me babysit for a little while."

Bracing herself, Catherine knelt beside Beth and looked at the tiny, squirming bundle. "She's beautiful."

Mark wandered a few feet away, propping his forearms on the back of an overstuffed chair, and tried to decipher the emotions chasing themselves across Catherine's face.

"I'd love to have a baby sister." Beth sighed. "Wouldn't it be fun to have a baby, CJ?"

"Babies are a lot of work, too," Catherine gently reminded her. It occurred to her that the dull ache she was accustomed to experiencing had curiously abated.

"Yeah, you're probably right. And since I don't have a mother," Beth continued wistfully, "I guess I won't get one any time soon."

Catherine chuckled at Beth's woebegone expression.

"Well, don't give up just yet. You never know what the future might bring."

Beth instantly brightened. "Hey, you're right! Maybe Daddy will marry someone and then we could have a baby."

We could have a baby. For some reason Mark had no difficulty envisioning Catherine pregnant. Where the image came from, he had no idea. It definitely wasn't something he routinely thought about when looking at a sexy woman. But somehow he knew that pregnant Catherine would be no less sexy, even on her way to the delivery room. The overpowering desire to see her in that condition left him shaken.

Catherine looked up from the baby to encounter Mark's enigmatic scrutiny. At his smokey gaze, sensual awareness surged through her. She jumped to her feet. "I think I'll see if Thelma needs help with dinner."

In that instant, the nebulous idea that had been floating around in Mark's head during his long, restless nights crystallized. He needed to begin his campaign. And time was limited.

Following her into the hallway, he captured her wrist in a determined grip. "Catherine?"

She didn't think she'd ever get used to hearing her name stroked in that uniquely intimate way of his. "Yes?"

"Go out with me tonight." She didn't miss the underlying urgency to the request.

She tugged against his hold. "Why?" His thinly veiled hunger stirred an answering hunger in her.

He didn't release her. "So skittish." Raising his free hand, he outlined her lower lip with the tip of one finger. The caress was feather-light. "Does there need to be a reason?" His tone was faintly chiding. Then he shrugged. "Okay. Because I want to repay you for what you've done for us. Because I like being with you. Because I need to discuss something with you. Will those do?''

She searched his face while fighting to contain an unfathomable longing. This time, she discovered, acquiescence came easier.

Studying Catherine from across the linen-clad dinner table, Mark wondered for the umpteenth time what it was that made her so sexually appealing to him. The dress she wore tonight was, as usual, conservative. But its fuchsia shade contrasted dramatically with her dark hair. And it was made of a fabric that enticed rather than revealed—that begged to be touched, intensifying that elusive promise of leashed passion.

His gaze drifted over her breasts. Small and firm, they would just fill a man's hands and leave him aching for more. There was no one part of her that had greater appeal than another. But the sum total, the whole of her, set him on fire. And sharpened his resolve to experience all of this inherently sensuous woman's secrets.

His steady stare was making her restless. Catherine took another sip of her wine. She knew she wasn't beautiful. Her bones were a little too sharp and didn't have quite enough padding. Her face, while not unattractive, had no outstanding feature. Neither tall nor short, she considered herself as just . . . average. She wondered what he saw when he inspected her as he was doing at that moment.

"How old are you, Catherine?"

She looked up from her menu, a bit startled. "Thirty-five. Well, actually closer to thirty-six." Mark was forever throwing her off balance with his from-out-in-left-field topics. "Why?"

He ignored her question. "You don't look it. In

fact, at times you look about sixteen.'' His eyes drifted over her with leisurely sensuality. ''Makes a great many of my thoughts about you illegal, if not downright immoral.''

In spite of her years of experience discouraging the opposite sex, Catherine felt heat rise in her cheeks. ''I thought we agreed not to do this,'' she countered, her voice strangled.

''This? This what? I distinctly remember agreeing not to kiss you again. And I've restrained myself. Just barely.'' He quirked an eyebrow, a smile hovering on his hard mouth. ''You said nothing about talking.''

That was true, she reminded herself sternly, attempting to recapture her composure. She was behaving like an adolescent. But how could she explain that his outrageous remarks—and her sexual reactions to them—were equally unsettling? And it wasn't just his remarks. It was unexpectedly looking up to catch him openly studying her, his eyes enigmatic. Or him simply touching her in some completely impersonal manner. Or any number of perfectly innocent incidents that nonetheless left her feeling as though she were riding a roller coaster minus an exit ramp.

He shrugged carelessly. ''Okay, if you don't like what I'm saying, then talk to me.''

''About what?'' she asked, taking what she hoped would be a calming sip of wine.

''Tell me about yourself. We've done a lot of talking about me and my problems while all I've gotten out of you is one very brief, cryptic summary.'' He settled back into the fan-back chair, obviously preparing to listen. ''Why don't you start with your practice.''

He appeared genuinely interested, and that surprised her. Most men, particularly outside the medical field, didn't relish talking shop with her. It made them uncomfortable, if not thoroughly intimidated. But Mark was equally confident discussing topics ranging from the mundane to the exceptional. It was only when the conversation became personal that he became uneasy. She could identify with that.

"What does a pediatric surgeon do?" he prompted, refilling her wineglass.

"Sees lots of kids." She laughed and began to relax for the first time since he'd picked her up that evening. Her practice was the center of her life, and she loved talking about it.

He smiled at her enthusiasm. "Why that particular field?"

"I love kids," she said simply. "Working with them is . . . rewarding. Especially the little ones. They're so innocent and untouched by life." From her chair beside the restaurant's balcony railing, she viewed the tiny, open courtyard below, filled with a profusion of greenery and tropical plants. She studied the tranquil scene a moment before continuing. "They haven't learned how to manipulate. And they appreciate what's done for them. I get such a sense of satisfaction when I'm able to help an injured child." She smiled self-consciously. "That sounds a bit egotistical, doesn't it?"

He shook his head. "Not at all." He liked watching her eyes light up as she talked. And he loved hearing her voice. Her faint, sweetly southern drawl, usually barely evident, became more audible when she was completely absorbed in her subject. He wondered what her voice would sound like while making love. Shifting uncomfortably, he hoped fervently he wouldn't have to wait too much longer to find out.

"I still don't understand why you don't have kids of your own. And don't you give me that bullsh— flip answer you gave me the other day on the beach."

Her eyes clouded momentarily and he watched her defenses slip into place. "Come on, Catherine. Don't close up on me now." He sensed the subject was forbidden, but he couldn't afford to leave it alone. "We've certainly discussed enough of my life," he reminded her. "Doesn't that entitle me to know something about you?"

Fortunately for Catherine the waiter appeared just then, giving her a few moments' reprieve.

When he'd left with their orders, she took a steadying breath. "I've had a child. She was born two and a half months premature and died minutes after her birth." Her voice had lost its soft inflection and taken on an impersonal edge. "It happened shortly after my divorce. My husband never knew I was pregnant." She regretted the disclosure immediately. She'd said more than she'd intended.

But revealing it to Mark hadn't caused the usual bittersweet sting. In fact, telling him made her feel as if she'd finally been relieved of a heavy burden. She found that somehow alarming.

"You're very good, Mark Garrett, at getting a woman to say more than she should. I don't usually bore people like this," she said disparagingly. *It must be the wine*, she thought. She wasn't used to drinking, and this was her second glass.

"Believe me, Catherine, I'm anything but bored." He studied her down-turned head as she distractedly rearranged her silverware, wishing he could see her expression. "Some women might consider it a blessing to lose the baby under those circumstances."

Catherine's head snapped up, her eyes murky with pain. "I can assure you I didn't." Even though her marriage had been a sham, she'd wanted her baby. Badly. After the loss, she'd thrown herself into her medical career and painstakingly walled off the deepest part of herself from further trauma. Until now.

He examined her face carefully. He recognized that she was still hiding secrets—secrets he needed to find out about. Soon. Secrets he knew caused her pain. Pain that he unaccountably wanted to banish. He didn't push her on the husband issue. He was relatively sure Catherine wasn't ready to talk about it. He didn't think he was ready to hear it.

Their meal of spicy curried chicken arrived. While the waiter unobtrusively arranged the condiments on their plates, Catherine used the few precious minutes to collect herself. When he finally withdrew, she was acutely conscious of the intimacy created by their large fan-back chairs. It was almost as if they were the only two people in the small, very exclusive night spot.

"You don't ever plan to have a child?" he asked before another thought struck him. "Or is it that you *can't*?"

"No." She answered the second question first. "Physically, I'm fine." From time to time the idea of having a child skirted around the edges of her thoughts. But Catherine shied away from single motherhood. She believed strongly that children needed two parents. That ruled out single-parent adoption or even artificial insemination. The other alternative, finding a man to accommodate her, threatened her hard-won emotional independence. The price, she'd decided long ago, was too great a risk. "I simply haven't chosen to try again."

"But you'd like to have a child of your own." It was more statement than question.

"Yes," she replied, her attention carefully focused on moving a forkful of curry-covered rice from one section of her plate to another. "I'm just not interested in the . . . complications connected with getting one."

Mark set down his fork and leaned back in his chair to lazily appraise her. "I've never heard it referred to in just those terms before," he remarked casually. "Dance with me, Catherine."

"Dance?" she asked blankly.

Mark stood, nodding in the direction of the small band which had begun to play soft Caribbean music. Without giving her an opportunity to decline, he eased her out of her chair and escorted her onto the minuscule dance floor.

He danced as he did everything else—with unwavering command. He folded her right hand against the heavy cadence of his heart and brought her lower torso into intimate contact with his. Like the primitive beat of the music, she felt the sensual connection all the way to her core.

He was reaching inside her and touching places no one had touched before. That tended to frighten her. But it didn't stop her body from adjusting to his like pieces of the same puzzle.

Raising her chin with one finger, he saw his own hunger reflected in her eyes. "It gets to you, doesn't it?" he murmured huskily, aligning her body so that she couldn't miss the hard outline of his arousal. "The chemistry between us is explosive."

She stiffened slightly, trying to counteract his seductive spell.

"Relax, Catherine, and go with it," he said, his voice exhibiting signs of strain. "Nothing can happen on a public dance floor." He hoped. Right at the moment, with the soft lantern light casting dim shadows and enveloping them in their own private world, he was having serious doubts.

Why not? a distant corner of her brain challenged daringly. Somehow dancing with Mark, her body locked to his, seemed so—she searched for the correct word—*familiar*.

He felt Catherine's body settle against his, and her small display of acceptance was the final straw. Releasing her abruptly, he said curtly, "Let's get the hell out of here. At least one of us needs to cool off."

Mark drove in brooding silence while Catherine pretended to concentrate on the silhouetted tropical foliage speeding past. Finally stopping at a deserted beach, he yanked the keys from the ignition and jerked open his door. "Let's walk."

Catherine had trouble keeping up. He covered the sandy ground in long, choppy strides, hands shoved deep into his pockets. The rigid set of his shoulders communicated his tension. After several long minutes his pace slowed, and he headed over to sit on a formation of volcanic rock, jutting onto the beach.

Something in his taut silence drew Catherine to sit closer than she ordinarily would have. A half-moon lent scant illumination to the scene, but it was enough to reveal his harsh features and eyes that reflected its cold light.

"I didn't kill my wife."

There was not the slightest hesitation before Catherine answered. "I didn't think you did."

Her unquestioning faith unleashed something in him that he was afraid to define, and he waited several moments before continuing. "Two months after our divorce became final, Elise died in an auto accident with one of her many male . . . friends." He paused again. "She was always too wild. Always wanted what she couldn't have and was never satisfied with what she had.''

Catherine couldn't miss the bitterness that shaded his words. He, apparently, considered himself in the unwanted category. Her heart twisted. ''You don't have to tell me this, Mark. It's none—''

''I have a reason,'' he interrupted. He didn't want to hear her say that this didn't concern her. ''Please.''

He waited for her nod of agreement. ''Her mother didn't want me to give her the divorce. Alice had never been able to control her daughter and expected me to ride herd on her and keep her out of trouble. When it became obvious even to me that keeping Elise out of trouble wasn't possible, I washed my hands of her. I knew that Alice blamed me for her death.'' He shook his head at his own stupidity. ''I should've suspected she'd eventually use that to turn Beth against me.''

''But she didn't succeed,'' Catherine quietly reminded him.

He didn't respond to her assurance. Instead he said, ''I have a proposition for you.'' He turned his head to study the miniature moonlit waves nuzzling the shoreline. ''Hear me out before you make a decision.''

It was just short of an order. His demeanor warned that one way or another he intended to have his say. ''All right.'' She sensed more than saw his rigid muscles relax.

''I want you to marry me.''

''Marry you?'' she repeated in patent disbelief. She was grateful for the semidarkness which acted as a partial shield and she hoped, helped hide her reaction. ''You can't be serious.'' She had an almost uncontrollable urge to laugh hysterically. Instead, she gripped a small protrusion of rock beside her as if it were the only reality in an otherwise irrational world. "I hate to sound clichéd, but we hardly know each other."

"Catherine." Though his voice remained neutral, the reminder was implicit.

She forced cool night air into her lungs and nodded once. "Go on."

"It's really quite logical. Marriage is a contract." He paused as if making sure she wasn't going to bolt. "I have certain needs you can fill. You have certain . . . needs I can fill. That's the purpose of a contract. Each side satisfies the needs of the other."

"Needs?" she echoed faintly, still reeling from the dispassionate proposal.

"I'll start with mine. This custody hearing is scheduled in two months. There's no question that I have to win."

At least on that point they were in agreement, Catherine thought a bit wildly. Over the last several days it had become almost as important to her as to Mark that he gain full custody of his daughter. She was convinced beyond doubt that was best, not only for Beth but for Mark as well. People who loved each other as these two did shouldn't be apart.

"You've been able to draw Beth out of her shell. Thanks to you, she's more open and relaxed with me than she's ever been." The sincerity in his simple statement touched her. Intuitively she understood how painful that must have been for him to admit.

Catherine shifted uneasily. Watching Mark and Beth grow closer over the last several days had soothed a part of her that had been raw for so long.

"At least she doesn't see me as the twenty-four-karat monster Alice describes." He raked the fingers of both hands through hair made midnight-black by the shadows. "But even though we're more comfortable with each other, we still have a long way to go."

Catherine was discovering something else about the pale darkness. It could expose emotions underlying what was said, subtle nuances conveyed in the words. She thought she detected an undertone of pleading, almost desperation, in Mark's, and she struggled to keep her own voice bland. "You're wrong, Mark. I may have been a catalyst, but she would have come around on her own. She loves you. You don't need me. You're doing fine."

"I don't have the luxury of time, Catherine. I need your influence now and until this court case is behind us."

"That wouldn't require marriage."

"If it were that simple." He climbed down from his position on the rocks. It served to put him in even closer proximity to her. "The court considers the home environment, too, and it doesn't look favorably on bachelor accommodations."

"You can't get married to satisfy the court," Catherine reasoned, having difficulty controlling the inner turmoil his logical arguments were creating in her.

"I'm thirty-seven, closer to thirty-eight." Catherine could just make out Mark's ironic half-smile as he mimicked her earlier words. "A man eventually needs the stability of one woman in his life, for companionship . . . among other things. Beth needs the security of a mother in hers. Marriage is the obvious solution."

It all sounded so . . . cold-blooded, she thought in desperation. "Well, I'm certainly not a viable choice."

"We haven't discussed how you would benefit from this arrangement."

"And how is that?" she challenged, recalling the pain and disillusionment of her first marriage.

He lowered himself onto the outcropping of rock beside her. "You want a baby," he reminded her with gentle candor. "And your biological clock is, as they say, ticking."

He'd managed to target one of her greatest concerns. Her chances of having a child of her own were quietly slipping away the longer she waited. In agitation she jumped down from her perch to stand a few feet away. "That may be true, but marriage isn't necessarily the answer."

"I see." His tone became cynical. "Planning on a few one-night stands?"

"Of course not!" Knowing his history she could understand his skepticism, but that he could think her capable of such conduct hurt unbearably. "Look, Mark." In self-protection, she crossed her arms over her breasts. "I have it on the very best authority that I'm not wife material."

He didn't think he was going to like her answer, but he asked anyway. "Whose?"

"My ex-husband." She felt chilled and turned her back to him, rubbing her arms for warmth. "You see, according to him, I'm not capable of pleasing a man or making one happy."

Reading between her delicately couched words, he cursed softly but eloquently. He'd like about ten minutes alone in some dark alley with her ex-husband.

"I was gullible enough once to believe marriage would work for me." Her voice reflected emptiness. "I don't care to repeat that mistake."

Squaring her shoulders, she faced him but didn't look at him directly. "Find another candidate." Her words were as cool and impersonal as the rocks she stood beside.

Her quiet dignity did almost as much to unsettle him

as the words themselves. Her mask was once again firmly in place. Mark expelled a frustrated breath. "If I had time, I'd prove to you how wrong you are. But time's the one thing I don't have."

Walking over to her, he settled his hands on her stiff shoulders. "You can't run from life forever, Catherine." He gave her a gentle shake, compelling her to look at him. "I'm not asking for love," he stated flatly, as if it were inconceivable that it would be offered even if he should ask.

"What I'm offering might not be perfect, but it's a damned sure way of giving us both what we need. I can't promise happiness. But I can promise to be the very best father I'm capable of being to any child we might have. And I can guarantee you financial security."

"I'm a realist, Mark, and I picture you being attracted to beautiful, sophisticated women." She gestured at her own body. "Not my category."

Her accuracy disturbed him, even though a short while ago he would have agreed with her. Now, the fact that she didn't recognize her own appeal to a man angered him. That, and the fact that he didn't want Catherine thinking him shallow or superficial.

The anger sharpened his words. "Maybe not, honey. But it's not their images I see when I close my eyes at night." He didn't bother to soften the crudity of his next remark. "It's you that's keeping me in a constant state of sexual arousal." His voice deepened and took on a husky edge. "Knowing you feel it, too, only adds to the agony." His fingers tightened on her shoulders, then eased fractionally. "Take my word for it, I won't have any trouble delivering my part of the bargain. And you won't have to worry about any other woman."

His blunt declaration sent fire racing to the lower region of her belly. "I can't instantly——" she had to swallow twice to get the words out "—make a decision like this."

The tension in him uncoiled marginally. She hadn't rejected him outright. "Beth and I have to leave for Atlanta tomorrow. There's a problem on one of the construction sites."

He captured her face between powerful hands that weren't quite steady and seductively rubbed her moist lower lip with one calloused thumb. "You've got two weeks."

The effect was no less potent than if he'd kissed her, and Catherine felt the impact all the way to her womb.

"God, baby," he groaned. The raw desire in her eyes was killing him. "Don't look at me like that." It was clear even in the dim light, though she was reeling from his proposition, that she wanted to be kissed as badly as he wanted to kiss her. "I gave you my word, Catherine," he reminded her roughly, urgency making his voice gritty. "If you've changed your mind, you'll have to tell me."

Catherine's gaze sought his mouth. All she had to do, she told herself, was lift hers just a few inches to again feel the explosive passion she'd experienced days earlier. But some inborn protective instinct held her frozen. Only her lips parted in silent invitation.

Her involuntary signal tightened the knot in his gut. "Just say it, sweetheart. I'll do the rest."

"Please," she whispered on a thread of sound.

It was the only verbal consent he needed. His mouth settled hungrily over hers, his hands holding her face captive and their bodies apart. If he didn't, they'd end up making love on the damp sand.

With difficulty he lifted his head and said harshly, "God, you can't ignore the sexual attraction between us. This alone would be enough to keep a man and woman bound for eternity.''

This time Catherine reached for his mouth, moaning low in her throat at the contact.

It took all his willpower to separate his mouth from her yielding kiss. ''Think about it carefully, Catherine,'' he told her gruffly, ''before you make your decision.''

FIVE

"So, what are you going to tell him?" Steve placed two bowls of conch chowder on the patio table and took his seat across from Catherine.

She smiled slightly, the brilliant midday sun reminding her that she'd left her dark glasses inside the villa. "I'm not sure."

"Not an unequivocal no. Well, that's progress, I guess," he teased lightly. "Does this mean you're considering his proposal?"

"You don't think it's a bit sudden?"

"Perhaps."

"Whose side are you on anyway?" Her voice held wry amusement.

"Oh, I'm not taking sides in this," Steve said philosophically. "I'm going to sit back and root for the winner."

"And wonder who that will be?" Catherine took a spoonful of the thick soup, barely tasting it. "Mark expects an answer when I get back to Atlanta."

He studied her distracted expression. "What's there

to lose if you accepted?'' Like the surgeon he was, Steve had a way of cutting through all extraneous material straight to the primary issue.

"My emotional independence?'' Catherine shrugged and pushed aside her unfinished soup. "I don't know. His proposition was so . . . impersonal.'' On some remote level she realized there was a contradiction here somewhere.

"Okay, let's take it from the other angle. What have you got to gain? I've known you far too many years not to recognize that your reactions to this guy and this situation are different. Besides, Mark Garrett impresses me as a man of his word.''

His endorsement of Mark surprised her. Catherine gave her good friend a meditative look. Though dispassionate, Mark's proposal *was* logical. And for some obscure reason she, like Steve, trusted him.

"Let's look at this objectively,'' Steve continued as he finished off his soup. "Even though you try hard to convince the world otherwise, you weren't cut out to be a nun, CJ. You're a warm, passionate woman who should've established another personal relationship long before now.''

"I've done okay.'' Catherine rose and began clearing the table.

Steve collected the remaining dishes and followed her from the patio into the cooler kitchen. "Ah, but you tell me you're not satisfied with 'okay' anymore. Right?''

Catherine didn't answer immediately. Instead, she busied herself with washing up their few lunch dishes, allowing her thoughts to analyze her situation. Lately she'd become acutely aware of the sterility of her life. Her medical practice had compensated for the loneliness until recently, but now it was becoming increasingly ineffective. For all her love of it, surgery tended to be an aloof specialty. Sometimes she felt as if she'd been lonely her entire life.

"Right," she finally conceded.

"You and Beth have formed a strong attachment in a very short time," Steve persisted.

"True." Watching Beth and Mark grow closer daily had given her such satisfaction. Being part of that process, Catherine had grown to love Beth with frightening speed and dreaded the possibility of severing all connections with the child. And she knew Beth would be hurt if she abruptly dropped out of her life.

"You'd like to have children of your own."

"Umm." Catherine's response was guarded. Even as well as he knew her, Steve probably didn't realize to what extent that was an understatement. She yearned to have a child of her own, to be able to shower him or her with all the love she had bottled inside her.

"Mother Nature won't wait around forever, you know." Steve continued his careful itemization. "And one thing's for certain. With the sparks that fly whenever you two are in the same room, there shouldn't be any problem in that department."

Which brought them to her greatest fear. She absently wandered onto the patio, stopping at the concrete railing to stare out at the harbor below. She idly watched the various sailing craft create random patterns in the sparkling water.

"But for how long?" she whispered softly.

Greg had been callously clear that being married to her left much to be desired. In fact, he'd systematically enumerated all her inadequacies as a wife and lover just before asking for a divorce so he could marry another woman. The woman, he'd added, who offered him all Catherine did not. The cruelty of her husband's rejection had convinced her that she had little to offer the opposite sex. She'd learned to protect herself from further pain by erecting impenetrable barricades around her emotions.

She had no doubt that once he gave his word, Mark would never retract it, and that once married, he would never desert her. But, without analyzing too closely the reason for her foreboding, she knew that witnessing Mark's desire turn to indifference would be more devastating than any previous rejection she'd experienced. Even if he never left her. Even if—or was that *particularly* if?—he spent the rest of his life with her.

Steve came up behind her and squeezed her shoulders. "CJ, you can't keep yourself walled off forever because of things that happened in the past," he said gently. "Sooner or later we all have to take chances."

"Dear Steve," Catherine said, patting his hand, "always trying to guide me in the right direction."

"I've seen you two together," he reminded her. "You're good for him. But more important, I think he'll be good for you." He gave her a hug. "Well, I've got to get back to the hospital. Think about it, CJ."

Catherine remained outside long after he'd gone, unconsciously enjoying the warm island breeze and thinking. Again Steve was right on target. At some point everyone had to take a chance, make a choice. She couldn't run from life forever. Mark's proposition, wrapped up in one tidy package, provided all she longed for in her life.

All, that is, but love, a tiny voice taunted. She shivered despite the sun's heat. Lightly running a finger over her lips, she vividly recalled the sexual impact of his kisses. Would a marriage built solely on practical needs protect her defenses and preserve her emotional independence? Could she keep her heart uninvolved?

But the most troubling question was—*did she want to?*

Mark rhythmically swung the blue-black iron sledge-hammer in lethal arcs, sending pebbles of concrete scattering several feet away. Work-honed muscles rippled with each hammer swing. Someone proving a critical point or alleviating severe frustration would not have exhibited more focused determination. The hot Georgia sun caused sweat to bead and glisten momentarily before running down his bare torso to be absorbed into the waistband of low-riding jeans. A Day-Glo yellow hard hat screened Catherine's presence from his view.

It was on his next upswing that he spotted her. His body stilled, and he slowly lowered the hammer, letting it drop unheeded to the ground. He stalked toward Catherine with purposeful strides and stopped within inches of her.

"I didn't expect you to come out to the site."

She savored his nearness and the musky odor of fresh male sweat. "I hadn't planned on it, but your office told me you were here." Catherine tried not to look at the perspiration tracks on his naked skin. It had been over two weeks since she'd last seen him, and she gripped her purse against the compulsive urge to follow those tracks with her fingers. "So I decided I'd like to see where you work," she finished lamely.

One side of his mouth lifted in a half-smile. "Yeah?" His eyes never leaving her, he pulled off one thick leather workglove and gestured toward the high-rise skeleton silhouetted at his back. "What do you think?"

"It's bigger than I imagined." She shifted uncomfortably under his unwavering scrutiny. He was squinting against the bright May light, making his eyes appear as dark slits behind his protective goggles.

"Look, if this is a bad time, I can leave." Her left hand worried at the strap of her suede shoulder bag. He wasn't making this easy. "Coming here wasn't a good idea. I'm sorry. I should have gotten in touch with you first." She realized she was babbling and decided an expedient departure might minimize what was becoming an awkward situation.

He caught her arm in a vise-like grip, his expression still unreadable. "No problem."

Without waiting for her consent, he directed her over to and through the door of a trailer situated next to the chain-link fence surrounding the property. His heavy workboots, dusted with red Georgia clay, resounded sharply on the equally dusty composition floor. Locating a blue chambray workshirt, he shrugged into it, leaving it hanging open to Catherine's hungry gaze.

"You'll need this." By way of explanation he positioned a yellow hard hat, similar to his own, on her head. He didn't immediately release the hat, in effect holding her hostage while he inspected each of her features minutely as if trying to delve behind them.

His impersonal touch sent a frisson of sexual excitement racing through her, and she inhaled sharply trying to steady her pulse. All that accomplished was to fill her senses with the essence that was uniquely his.

"Come on." His hands left her, and he stepped away. His voice was as impersonal as his touch had been. "I'll give you our VIP tour."

She could no longer see his eyes, hidden now by mirrored sunglasses he'd substituted for the safety goggles, and had no clue to his thoughts.

"Thank you." It seemed the most prudent remark at the moment.

The tour was quick but thorough. Mark introduced her to his work crew, made up of the customary number of men, but which also included several women in key positions. An unexpected smattering of young people Catherine judged to be in their mid to late teens watched her with obvious curiosity. Though he treated everyone in the same reserved manner, each person she met showed genuine respect and admiration for Mark Garrett.

He saved for last a breathtaking view of the Atlanta skyline from atop the partially finished structure. The entire procedure, from beginning to end, had been conducted with the same businesslike manner that he'd displayed since her arrival.

As their construction elevator slowly descended, Catherine was again acutely conscious of Mark's scrutiny from behind his dark glasses.

"Your company seems to be handling the recession well," she commented to fill the silence and ease her growing nervousness.

"It's holding its own."

The elevator finally reached ground level and creaked to a stop.

"Okay, Catherine. We've done the social bit." He slid open the bulky safety gate. "Why are you here?"

The directness of the question, as usual, threw her. "Could we talk somewhere a little more private?"

He became motionless for a moment, then shrugged. He steered her across the construction site and again into the trailer. Two workmen, poring over what appeared to be blueprints, seemed to sense they weren't welcome and quickly departed.

Once alone, Mark removed his dark glasses. Bracing narrow hips against one of the cluttered desks, he folded his arms across his chest. "I'm listening."

This was going to be more difficult than she'd envisioned. She removed her hard hat and carefully hung it on a wallpeg near the door. "I've—" Catherine cleared her throat once, glanced around the small office, and began again "—I've decided to accept your offer."

Something flared in the clear depths of his eyes but was extinguished before she could define it. "Let's go" was all he said.

"Do you mind telling me where?" she challenged in mild exasperation.

"My house." His answer was terse. "We need to talk someplace we won't be disturbed."

His cryptic mood was making Catherine uneasy. Somehow she'd expected a slightly different reception to her announcement. After all, the proposal *had* been his idea. Trying to quiet the burgeoning doubts, she followed Mark to a large pickup. He opened a door with the words Garrett Construction discreetly stenciled on its side and helped her navigate the rather high step up to the passenger seat. His face was still set in taut lines as he tossed his hard hat into the backseat and climbed behind the wheel.

Short of the weather or the scenery, about the only topic Mark would willingly discuss during the ride was Beth, and that was done sketchily. Having gleaned that his daughter was physically well and with her grandmother until the weekend, Catherine finally fell silent.

They'd left most of the city's congestion behind and were heading into the more sparsely populated region north of Atlanta when Mark turned the truck onto a private drive.

Though not ostentatious, the house that came into view was nonetheless impressive. Its contemporary lines blended into the surrounding native trees and rocky landscape, creating a compatible effect that invited the observer to linger and enjoy.

Inside, Mark ushered her into a moderate-size office only slightly less cluttered than the one at the construction site. He went straight to a phone on his desk, impatiently punching in the numbers. "I need to see you," he told the person on the other end. There was a brief pause, then, "Right. As soon as you can. Thanks, Paul."

He hung up and turned to Catherine. "I'm going to grab a quick shower. Make yourself at home. Feel free to look around."

"Fine," Catherine said to the now-empty doorway, "I'll do that."

Relieved at having their discussion temporarily postponed, she wandered through the ground floor. The interior of the house was as impressive as its exterior. Cathedral ceilings and enormous, unadorned windows provided spaciousness while seeming to bring nature right into each room. The effect was soothing, if a touch austere.

Her impression of Mark's home was definitely not that of a bachelor's quarters. It would require only minor touches to add the needed warmth. She decided it must be an exceedingly pleasant place to live.

Mark located Catherine fifteen minutes later in the great room overlooking the secluded back grounds. With her attention captured by the view, he could study her unobserved. She'd pulled her hair into a controlled topknot that subdued its shimmering highlights. Decked out in her usual sedate attire, she was wearing off-white slacks and a silky cinnamon-colored blouse, buttoned all the way to her throat.

The temptation to put his hands on her, to map what

lay hidden beneath, was not diminished by the prim effect. He'd never known a woman who could turn him on as fast—or with the same gut-level intensity—as Catherine. With difficulty he suppressed the urge.

First they would talk.

Again he struggled with the burgeoning apprehension. She'd said she was going to accept his proposal, he reminded himself and started toward her.

When she sensed his presence behind her at the huge window, Catherine started but recovered quickly. "Your home is magnificent." Genuine pleasure sparkled in her eyes. "Did you design it?"

He hesitated. "Yes, thanks."

"Of course." Catherine was almost apologetic. "That wasn't very bright of me. You must design all your buildings."

"No. I have a team of architects who does that." Something undefinable moved in his face—a battle between two strong emotions. His gaze circled the room, touching on the heavy cedar beams spanning the high ceiling and the sculptured stairway curving to the second floor, before returning to her. He smiled but it didn't reach his eyes. "This was just a diversion."

"You're joking, right?"

His grim expression answered for him.

Of course he's not, she thought sadly. He'd never admit to being corrupted by artistic talent. Not after having endured his mother's abuse of her own talent. Her heart turned over at the thought.

"Forget I said anything," she amended and changed the subject. "You said you wanted to talk?"

"Have a seat." He sprawled into an overstuffed armchair that should have looked out of place in the ultramodern room but didn't.

Choosing to sit across from him on a suede sofa at

right angles with the tranquil window view, she waited for him to begin.

"You're agreeing to marry me?" His voice was as bland as his expression.

Catherine inclined her head the slightest degree before answering. "Yes." Her uneasiness returned. "Look, Mark, if you've changed your mind, just say so. I promise I won't become hysterical."

That's what he figured. "I haven't changed my mind." He carefully steepled his fingers and regarded her intently. "What will you get out of it?"

Startled by the question, she challenged, "I thought we went over all that in St. Croix. Why do it again?"

He shook his head slowly from side to side. "I pointed out the advantages of this arrangement for each of us. You had strong reservations." His gaze remained steady. "Talk to me."

Agitated, Catherine left her seat and paced to the window. She wasn't prepared to discuss her reasons for accepting his proposal. He didn't press, but she remained conscious of his patient regard.

"I expect the customary things anyone expects from marriage," she said finally. "Companionship, stability—a family."

"And your reservations, Catherine," he repeated. "Have you resolved them?"

She faced him with eyes that now snapped with self-protective anger. "Not all of them, no." His continued pursuit of this was making her defensive. "But I've decided that the positives outweigh the negatives in this arrangement." She hated that word. It was so—impersonal.

"I want no misunderstandings between us. What's still bothering you?"

Catherine felt a renewed flutter of unease. He wasn't

going to let the subject rest. She might as well get it over with.

"As I told you before, I don't fare too well with relationships. There seems to be something lacking in me."

"Don't," he commanded quietly, "belittle yourself." He hated hearing her say anything derogatory about herself.

She paused, surprised at his vehemence. She hadn't intended to sound self-pitying. Her basic sense of honesty—and self-protection—demanded that she state the facts as she saw them. "Learning to be emotionally independent was a long, hard fight. It's very important to me. Becoming dependent on someone again tends to frighten me."

A nameless emotion knifed into Mark, but he ruthlessly pushed it aside.

Unfolding from his chair, he started toward her. "That's the beauty of this arrangement. Your . . . independence won't be affected." The taut set of his mouth contradicted the blasé stroll which brought him to her side. "Our marriage will be based on mutual respect and mutual needs. We don't need the illusion of love." He was well acquainted with its treachery. He would never give that weapon to another woman.

"I don't expect it from you," he assured her bluntly. "Don't expect it from me."

"I see." At least he was meticulously honest, she reasoned, attempting to dilute the cold, empty feeling invading her. She recalled his statement about love at the time he'd proposed and realized now, too late, that she'd misinterpreted his meaning. "I hadn't considered that you meant to exclude even the . . . possibility of love."

Her stricken expression and too-quiet voice bothered

him in a way he couldn't define, making his words harsher than he'd intended. "On St. Croix I told you I wasn't asking for love. It's nothing more than subterfuge. It lures the poor sucker who believes in it into a false sense of security." *And left the bastard defenseless against its destructive force.*

"I see," Catherine repeated. He should have explained the rules sooner. Now was too late. The pain twisting her heart confirmed what she'd begun to fear.

She already loved Mark Garrett.

The realization left her dazed, and she struggled to sort out the turbulent thoughts careening through her mind. He hadn't offered his love to begin with, she reminded herself firmly. His denouncement of it now didn't change anything. The proposition remained just as it was when she decided to accept it. But having acknowledged her love for him, could she survive the certainty of never having his?

"I won't let you back out now, Catherine." Fear traced a cold path down his spine, and he cursed fluently under his breath. "We have everything we need for a mutually satisfying marriage."

It had taken her hours of soul-searching and nights of sleeplessness to reach that same conclusion. She would not change her mind.

"I realize that." She spoke very softly while the question resounded shrilly in her head: *But what about love?*

Her words did little to reassure Mark, and a compulsion to erase her anguished look tore at him. He reached for her, pulling her against his body with a strength born of desperation.

"Say it." He claimed her mouth with his, then lifted his head just enough to grate out, "Say you'll marry me."

This time Catherine didn't hesitate. She accepted his rough kiss hungrily, craving the reassurance that, if nothing else, he wanted her physically.

Mark knew the exact instant her fragile defenses crumbled. The knowledge was as potent as an aphrodisiac. He stepped into the breach, aligning her body to his with hands that shook with the need clawing at him.

Inundated by his unrestrained passion, she had to fight for breath and the fraction of space required to answer him. "I told you, Mark," she whispered, her voice unsteady, words slurred, "I keep my word."

He answered with a guttural groan and again slanted his mouth over hers, this time demanding entrance. Her uninhibited response seriously undermined his tenuous self-control. Catherine wasn't a virgin, but apparently she was incredibly inexperienced in dealing with an aroused male. The bolt of lightning that thought ignited went straight to his gut.

Only with great effort did he lift his head to scan her flushed features. "You don't have any idea how rare this is, do you?" He laughed hoarsely. "Or how bad you make me want you."

She knew, in some dark recess of her mind, that Mark would stop instantly if she gave the slightest indication that she wasn't amenable to what he was doing to her. But she didn't consider resisting. Instead, she avidly encouraged him. Pushing her body against his and planting her fingers in his hair, she anchored his mouth to hers.

The heat was overwhelming. He released her mouth and moved down her throat to her breast in a futile attempt to cool the flames or at least to temper them. The damp spot he created on her silk blouse clung lovingly to the erect tip. *God, she was hot—so hot. And so sweet.* The contrast was devastating.

Some saner corner of his brain warned he was losing what little control he had left. And being grossly unfair to Catherine. The realization angered him. He prided himself on never losing control with a woman. Particularly where sex was concerned.

"Easy, sweetheart." The words sounded rusty. His legs weren't going to support him much longer. He could not take her, he warned himself. Some primal instinct told him he didn't dare until he had her irrevocably tied to him. Pulling Catherine over to the sofa, he sat in one corner and settled her across his lap with the intention of gentling her down from the erotic high.

Catherine moaned low in her throat and sought his mouth. He clamped down hard on the temptation to take what she was so generously offering, but her restless movements were bringing her into intimate contact with his aching erection. If he didn't do something soon, he was going to explode like an untried teenager.

Moving her away a few inches, he unbuttoned her blouse and fumbled with her bra. When he brushed the material aside, he caught his breath. She was exquisite. Each dusky-rose nipple was knotted with arousal and begging for attention. He rubbed calloused thumbs over the tips, her responsive moan stoking his own arousal.

He knew better than to allow things to go this far when he had no intention of finishing them. Dropping his head back against the sofa, he struggled against the urgency consuming him. Well, he could end her torment if not his own. He owed her that much.

Drawing a steadying breath, he whispered huskily, "Easy, baby. Let me take care of you." Undoing the opening to her slacks, he eased his hand inside her bikini briefs until he found the warm cleft at the apex of her legs. She was wet and welcoming, and writhed at his intimate touch.

Catherine was completely immersed in the sensual spell Mark was weaving. She wanted simultaneously to speed up and slow down what he was doing to her. She was certain she didn't want him to stop. Craving something . . . more, she arched against his hand. As if he recognized her need, she felt his finger seek then find her hidden, sensitized flesh.

The breathy little sounds she was making were about to push Mark over the edge. He raised his head to look at her. Fully aroused she was stunning, and he realized he could too easily become addicted to her wild abandon. Ever so slightly increasing the pressure, he again caressed the slick nubbin.

Watching Catherine through eyes hazed with his own passion, he delicately stroked—once . . . twice . . . and again, until he felt the beginnings of her soft convulsions. Stilling his hand, he dragged air into his oxygen-starved lungs and held her tightly while she rode out the sensual storm.

As Catherine fought to catch her breath, Mark tenderly cradled her head against his shoulder and savored the primitive satisfaction that he could bring her to this level of pleasure. Though his own body still screamed for release, he garnered some gratification in knowing that at least momentarily hers did not.

Catherine felt betrayed—along with the first inkling of apprehension. If he wanted her so badly and found her so sexually appealing, why had he denied himself the fulfillment she had eagerly offered? His restraint made her wanton behavior seem almost . . . sordid, and she felt her face heat with embarrassment.

Without lifting her head from his shoulder, she finally asked, "Why?"

Mark tensed. He should have expected her to question his motives for stopping short of complete intimacy. But he wasn't prepared to answer.

The doorbell pealed into the lengthening silence.

"There wasn't time," he said, seizing the fortuitous interruption. He'd have to remember later to thank Paul for his punctuality. "Why don't you go freshen up?" he suggested, his voice sounding rusty to his own ears.

He wasn't about to tell her the real reason for denying himself the pleasure of her body—that he feared becoming addicted before securing the source.

Catherine raised her head then, confirming that he looked as composed as he sounded. The observation didn't help reduce her growing uncertainty.

Again the doorbell intruded.

"Go on, sweetheart," Mark urged softly when she continued to hesitate, "you'll feel better. Upstairs, last door at the end of the hall." He gently straightened her clothes enough for her to stand, then helped her to her feet. "When you're ready, come back down. I want you to meet someone."

Summoning what dignity she could muster, Catherine ascended the stairs, wondering if it were possible to ever rebuild her own composure. Finding the master suite, she noticed that it was indelibly stamped as Mark's, the furniture large, expensive, and built for comfort—and sensual pleasure. The latter observation only added to her growing doubts. In the bathroom, she splashed cool water on her face. It didn't help, she realized, studying her flushed features in the mirror above the ceramic sink.

Remembering her uninhibited behavior of only moments before, she cringed. She'd thought their arousal mutual. Had she been wrong? He'd had little difficulty reining in his own desire. If he found her as sexually appealing as he claimed, why hadn't he made love to her? Actually, he had, she reminded herself bluntly. It was he who had been denied release.

Taking another look at herself in the mirror, she noticed that her eyes were still dilated, and all the water in the Arctic couldn't cool her heated face. With Mark and a guest waiting downstairs, now wasn't the time to analyze her feelings. Quickly she smoothed her hair, squared her shoulders, and left the room.

As Mark watched Catherine descend the stairs, the first thing he noticed was her cool reserve. The well-loved, vulnerable expression she'd worn only a short while ago was now wiped clean. Something raged in him at the thought. He wanted to drag her to the nearest bed—hell, the damned floor would do—and restore her earlier softly tousled look.

Remembering Paul's presence, he settled instead on pulling her possessively against his side. But she held herself stiffly, all her earlier yielding gone.

As soon as the necessary introductions were completed, Catherine eased from his hold and escaped to a nearby chair. She couldn't bring herself to sit on the sofa. All her uncertainties didn't dilute the memory of what had transpired there only a short time ago. She felt her stomach flutter and heat pool in the lower region of her pelvis. Drawing a deep breath, she forced herself to concentrate on what was being said.

Paul Martin was not what Catherine expected. The comfortable camaraderie between Mark and his attorney spoke of deep mutual respect and understanding.

"I've arranged for Judge Johnston to marry you in his chambers this Saturday," Paul informed them matter-of-factly. He was also, it appeared, very efficient.

"That soon?" Catherine realized she probably wasn't doing a very good job of disguising her dismay.

"Mark said he wanted it done ASAP." Paul gave Catherine a sympathetic look that signaled he was well acquainted with his friend's sometimes arrogant tactics. "Is there a problem?"

"There's no problem," Mark answered for her. Cool gray eyes seemed to dare Catherine to dispute him. "She knows the reason for this marriage and how critical it is that it be done quickly. Don't you, Catherine?"

"Saturday will be fine, Paul," she assured him just as coolly. What difference did it make, she reasoned, how soon they married? Her decision was made.

"Good." Paul seemed relieved. "I have some forms you need to fill out. Do you intend to keep your surname after you're married, Catherine?"

Her first reaction was to tell Paul that she wanted to take her husband's name. Her eyes shifted from Paul to Mark. His expression remained bland, as if he could care less one way or the other. A nebulous hope withered before being fully formed. Perhaps by keeping her name she could protect a small portion of her independence—and ultimately her heart.

"Since I'm already established in the professional community under Chambers, it seems the . . . best solution."

Mark was surprised at the possessive anger her answer kindled in him and used that anger to mask his apprehension.

He was only marginally reassured that Saturday was only a few days away.

SIX

From Judge Johnston's sixth-floor courthouse window, Catherine surveyed the street below filled with soggy Saturday afternoon traffic and wished, for the hundredth time in a handful of days, that Steve was here to give her some of his straight-for-the-jugular advice. She certainly could use it. But he hadn't been able to get away on such short notice to attend the wedding. Along with his love he'd sent his best wishes and the advice to go for it.

The fact that she loved Mark Garrett was still new—and frightening. An emotional chasm yawned between them, and she wondered if it could ever be bridged. Pressing one hand against her stomach, she tried to control the keen edge of panic. Was she doing the right thing? Or was she foolishly committing herself to long-term heartache?

"Okay, have you got everything? Something old, new, borrowed, and blue?" Lynn Henderson's amused voice intruded into Catherine's deliberation.

"I think so," Catherine answered distractedly, fingering the ivory crepe de chine dress she wore.

116

Thank God for Lynn. She was a colleague and, though she hadn't shared Catherine's traumatic past as Steve had, was a good friend. The need for haste had left little time for planning. Catherine had barely had enough time to move her possessions from her small house to Mark's and take care of the most pressing business details, let alone plan a wedding. When told it was to be a simple civil ceremony, Lynn had insisted on providing at least a few of the traditional trappings.

Catherine recognized that she was probably being overly sentimental in wanting at least some of the trimmings of a real wedding. Time was of the essence in their situation. Still, that didn't stop the feeling of disappointment that Mark didn't seem to feel the same loss.

"It's a shame Beth couldn't attend the wedding."

Catherine turned away from the window and watched Lynn fuss with her compact mirror. She, too, wished Beth was here. "Under the circumstances, this—" she waved her hand to encompass all that was to take place shortly "—is the best way."

Her friend nodded in agreement as she tried to tame a stray wisp of hair.

Though understanding the need for caution, Catherine still felt she should justify the decision. "Mark was concerned about how Beth's grandmother would react if she discovered our plans before the wedding. And it would've been very difficult for Beth to keep this secret."

"You're right, of course," Lynn said, glancing at Catherine. "It's just that I'm looking forward to meeting Beth. She sounds adorable."

Catherine smiled, thinking of Beth. "She is that. But Mark said that the judge wants to discuss the details of the custody hearing today. That would be awkward with Beth here.''

Lynn put away her compact and leveled a reassuring gaze on the nervous bride. ''Honey, everything's going to work out just fine. You'll see.''

She prayed her friend was right.

A discreet knock at the door heralded Paul Martin's arrival. He took a long look at Catherine and released a low whistle of approval. ''Mark sent me ahead with this,'' he said, handing her a florist's box.

Inside, blood-red roses contrasted dramatically with the palest of creams, the bold effect softened by baby's breath and off-white netting. Not the usual bridal corsage, she noted with some misgiving. The enclosed card stated simply: *To my lady of fire and ice. Mark.* The whimsical gesture, coming from this particular man, touched her far more than any traditional symbol possibly could have. She hugged the thought close.

''What an interesting color choice,'' Lynn observed as she efficiently pinned the flowers at Catherine's shoulder, then stepped back to admire her handiwork. ''There. You look perfect.''

''I'll second that,'' Paul agreed readily.

''Thank you.'' Catherine wondered if she sounded as unsteady as she felt.

''Well, I'm off to find the ladies' room,'' Lynn announced. ''See you in a few.''

''Quite a man, our Mark,'' Paul commented after the door closed behind the other woman. ''He can be amazingly insensitive at times. If you haven't already guessed, it's a protective mechanism.''

Still not trusting her voice, Catherine nodded. Paul's shrewd eyes apparently hadn't missed her reaction, but he'd misinterpreted what he saw.

''He's a loner. Seldom opens up to anyone,'' he continued. "I've known him for a good many years, and in some ways he's still a mystery."

"I can believe that." Catherine's slight smile was ironic as she recalled how close-mouthed Mark could be about himself. "I've noticed he gives away not one fact more than is absolutely necessary."

"That lesson came early in his life. On the streets you learn quickly and well—if you want to stay alive."

Catherine shuddered at the images Paul's words evoked.

"Has he told you about Joe?"

"Yes, some. Enough for me to know that he meant a great deal to Mark."

Paul nodded. "His teen years were brutal. By the time Joe found him, Mark was surviving by his wits alone. Joe managed to keep him from making some bad mistakes."

"I gathered as much from what little he did tell me." Her heart bled for what a young Mark must have endured. "Thank God for Joe."

"Yeah." Paul echoed her sentiments. "Joe came along at a critical time. But don't believe for a minute that Mark owes his success to anyone other than himself."

Catherine agreed with that. She knew firsthand how determined and single-minded Mark Garrett could be. And what kind of fighter he was. The only catalysts he needed were the harsh experiences life handed him.

"I guess what I'm trying to say is that Mark's a good man. You'll never find one better. But living with him won't be easy." Paul's warning was edged with empathy. "He runs deeper than he wants anyone to know."

His words seemed to hold some unspoken message,

but Catherine didn't have a chance to decode it as Lynn breezed back in.

"I believe the groom has arrived," she announced.

As if on cue, Mark strolled into the room.

Lynn squealed, "You can't come in here!"

At the same time Paul protested, "Hey, wait a minute, good buddy!"

Neither deterred Mark.

Catherine's heart skittered. Dressed in a dark-gray business suit he looked even more formidable than usual. Yet he wore it, she decided, with the same ease he wore his more casual clothing. His gaze connected with hers, quickly skimmed the length of her, then more slowly retraced its path. Though his expression was unreadable, a sensual current arced between them.

Lynn tried unsuccessfully to jostle Mark back out the door. "You're not supposed to see the bride before the ceremony! Don't you know it's supposed to be bad luck?" she demanded in feigned exasperation.

Mark was anything but superstitious. He knew a man made his own luck. Even so, something in the good-natured warning bothered him. He studied Catherine's face. Her sherry-brown eyes were overly bright with mild uncertainty and something else he couldn't quite identify.

Uneasiness stirred in him. Again Mark recalled her decision not to take his name, and uneasiness expanded into an indefinable apprehension. Did her decision indicate a lack of commitment, a lack of permanence on her part? His concern, either way, made him angry.

"But we don't believe in trivial sentiment, do we, Catherine?" he challenged quietly. Ignoring the others, he sauntered across the room to stop in front of her. "The judge is ready to talk to us about the custody hearing."

"Couldn't that wait until after the ceremony?" Lynn grumbled to no one in particular.

"No." The word held absolute finality. Holding Catherine's gaze, Mark lightly ran his fingers down her arm to capture her hand in his. "After the wedding we have other business to take care of."

His meaning wrapped around Catherine and heated more than just her cheeks. "It's fine, Lynn. Don't worry about it."

Mark's hard mouth softened fractionally at her discomfort. "Come on," he said gently, ushering her toward the door. "Harold's waiting for us."

"I'm afraid I don't understand this, Judge Johnston." Catherine leaned forward in her chair, intently studying the white-haired man seated behind the enormous desk. "Doesn't a father have a stronger legal right to custody than a grandmother?"

"Please, call me Harold," he said, giving her a reassuring smile. "And to answer your question, yes, usually. But in Beth's case there are extenuating circumstances."

"Such as?" Catherine asked, still confused.

"Such as the fact that Alice believes I'm a bastard not fit to have anything to do with her granddaughter." In frustration Mark jerked himself from his chair beside Catherine and strode to the window to stare out at the rain-washed buildings across the street.

"Mark," the older man chided, a soft reprimand in his tone. "Catherine's entitled to a little more explanation than that."

"Right." Keeping his back to them, Mark sighed and dragged a hand through his hair. "Alice believes the only way to save Beth is by taking her away from me." He laughed bitterly. "It never occurred to me that leaving Beth with her grandmother in the first place would turn out to be such a stupid mistake. I knew the woman had little use for me. But I never imagined her hatred for me would drive her to turn my daughter against me. It's no surprise that Beth wonders if I'm some kind of monster.''

The pain in his words slashed at Catherine's heart. "Mark, you know Beth doesn't believe that."

An almost imperceptible flexing of his tense shoulders was the only indication that Mark had heard her gentle rebuke.

"In a custody fight," Harold explained, taking up the legal implications in Mark's terse recitation, "the court looks at all aspects of a child's life. In this case, because of Alice's hostility, Beth feels, shall we say, uncomfortable around Mark."

"Uncomfortable, maybe," Catherine conceded, not hiding her frustration at the unfairness of the situation, "but she still loves her father very much."

"That, of course, will be taken into account," the judge said. "But you must remember that no matter what Alice feels toward Mark, she does love her grandchild. And Beth loves her."

Mark was relieved to have Joe's old friend finish explaining the facts of the case to Catherine. Harold probably figured it was safer for his furnishings. The frustrated anger eating at Mark made him want to smash something.

He would do whatever was necessary to keep Beth. Anything. He remembered all too vividly the devastation of a parent's desertion. He'd make damned sure his daughter never knew that despair. He'd learned on the streets how to survive—and win. He'd find a way now.

"Cut to the chase, Harold." Mark swung around to

face them. "In addition to those 'minor' problems, my lifestyle hasn't been what the court would consider family oriented."

His gaze collided with Catherine's. "That's why marrying you is so important."

For a split second she glimpsed something raw, and it was almost more than she could bear. But his words were a harsh reminder of the real reason he was marrying her. Something in her rebelled at his making their marriage sound nothing more than practical. "What happens next?"

"Sometime before the hearing a court-appointed psychologist will talk with all concerned parties," Harold said. "His or her recommendations will be given careful consideration."

Mark made an inarticulate sound, his rigid stance communicating clearly how much he hated being at the mercy of others. A cold feeling of dread slithered through Catherine. What if this didn't work out? What if, after all their efforts, the court still awarded custody to Beth's grandmother?

"Tell her what makes up a favorable report," Mark ordered grimly, spreading his suit jacket and jamming his hands into the pockets of his slacks. He already knew.

"Evidence of a good working relationship between father and daughter. A stable home environment. A cohesive family unit." Harold slowly and precisely ticked each item off.

"As you can see, we've got our work cut out for us." With decisive steps Mark walked over to Catherine and held out one work-toughened hand. "Ready?" His eyes, usually steely gray, softened fractionally as his gaze swept over her upturned face.

She hesitated the merest fraction of a second. Here

was her last chance to say no, to preserve her safe emotional fortress. Before the thought was fully formed she discarded it.

"Yes," she answered, and placed her hand in his.

Mark's hand absorbed the faint trembling in hers. Could he trust Catherine? Or would she ultimately betray him as every other female in his life had?

Even with Harold presiding and Paul and Lynn witnessing, the civil ceremony seemed brief and impersonal. How could something that perfunctory be legally binding? Catherine wondered. And what about emotionally? She shivered.

Maybe a marriage with no promise of love would be ultimately less painful. If she expected nothing, she silently reasoned, she couldn't be disappointed.

She touched the recent addition to the third finger of her left hand. Had Mark known, when he picked this particular ring, that a plain gold band would be the least intrusive to her work? Because her hands were the tools of her profession, she seldom if ever wore jewelry. Had he thought of that? Or had he simply purchased the simplest item available?

Either way, she was just as married.

Catherine wasn't expecting to find the house empty when they arrived home later that evening. She looked questioningly at Mark. "Where's Beth?"

He finished removing his tie and worked open several buttons of his shirt. A faint smile touched his hard mouth. "This is our wedding night." He returned her look with eyes that had deepened to dark charcoal. "I want no distractions. Do you?"

Catherine's stomach fluttered alarmingly at the sensual challenge. She found holding his direct stare difficult, but she didn't hedge her answer. "No."

"Good." Her honesty when dealing with personal issues impressed—and surprised—him. He walked over to a wet bar hidden in an alcove formed by the curving staircase. "Would you like a drink?"

She shook her head. She wanted nothing that would dull what was to come. She might be nervous, but she wanted to experience every subtle nuance of it. She intended to gather as many memories as possible before what desire Mark felt for her waned.

He poured himself a healthy amount of Scotch. "Hungry?"

Again she shook her head. *Not for food.* "I'm still stuffed from the marvelous meal at the restaurant."

Now *that* was a lie, Mark thought. She'd barely touched her food. He wondered if she had any idea how fragile she looked in her white dress with her hair softly framing her face. For someone who had been married before, she was extremely naive when it came to the effect she had on a man. He took a healthy swallow of Scotch.

"Sit down, Catherine. I'm not going to pounce on you." His words were ironic since that was exactly what he ached to do. Since he'd known this woman he'd been in an almost constant state of arousal. But as badly as he wanted her at this precise moment, he knew he needed to cool down. Otherwise their first time together would be too hot. Too intense. Too . . . consuming.

The *wanting* he could handle, he told himself. But he would not allow this physical craving for her to turn into *need*. That he must never permit.

Catherine almost obediently dropped onto the leather sofa, acutely conscious of the violent fires that burned in Mark's eyes and of what had happened the last time she sat here.

Breaking the visual connection, Mark prowled the room for several long minutes. "Beth's with her grandmother," he commented, finally answering Catherine's earlier question. "We'll pick her up tomorrow afternoon."

"I'm anxious to see her again." *Brilliant conversation!* Catherine thought in self-mockery, but for the life of her, she could think of nothing more imaginative to say.

Mark watched Catherine finger her wedding ring and unconsciously touched his own bare ring finger. What was she thinking? He cursed the circumstances that prohibited them from even briefly getting away together. But the impending custody battle hadn't allowed them the time. How many women, he wondered, would get married for the sake of another woman's child and not scream bloody murder when they didn't get a honeymoon? None in his experience came to mind.

Except Catherine.

With deliberate care Mark set his glass on the nearest table, crossed the room, and pulled Catherine into his arms. "We have tonight," he stated gruffly, "and I intend to make the most of it."

"Yes," she agreed unsteadily an instant before his mouth settled over hers. He stirred sensations in her she'd never known existed and wasn't sure she wanted. On some level, they bewildered her. Made her feel as if he were dismantling her protective shell layer by layer.

Mark's brain kept cautioning temperance, but Catherine's uninhibited response rekindled the fires he had so determinedly banked. His desire for this woman was like a savage beast relentlessly testing the constraints of its cage.

His hands impatiently molded her body to his, then cupped the gentle curve of her behind and brought her fully into the cradle of his thighs. When Catherine's hips sweetly pushed against his, he groaned heavily. A distant voice chided that he was again—and too damned easily—losing control.

The jarring ring of the telephone penetrated the sensual haze enveloping them. Mark swore eloquently before releasing Catherine.

As soon as he answered the phone and handed it to Catherine he knew the evening was over. A part of him rejoiced. It gave him the precious time he needed to get a stronger grip on his self-control.

"I'm needed at the hospital," Catherine explained as she replaced the receiver minutes later. "A young boy I operated on yesterday is showing signs of internal bleeding." She had the sinking feeling that something more than their lovemaking had been interrupted. "I'm sorry."

"Don't apologize, Catherine." His voice still held the grittiness of arousal. "Go get changed."

In the master bedroom, as she quickly stripped out of her dress and into slacks and a blouse, she analyzed Mark's reaction. Would most men be so complacent at having their wedding night disturbed? A tiny doubt niggled. Had he been relieved?

She couldn't dwell on that disturbing thought now, she told herself, racing back downstairs.

Mark met her at the foot of the stairs. "Ready?"

She absently noticed that he, too, had changed into worn jeans and denim jacket. "Yes, as soon as I get my car keys."

"I'll take you," he said, ushering her toward the door to the garage.

His offer caught her by surprise. "You don't have to do that."

Mark glanced at her with eyes that glittered warningly. "Have you looked outside recently?" he asked softly, drawing her attention to the torrential downpour that hadn't abated since early afternoon.

"I wouldn't let any woman, let alone my wife—" he felt an unexpected surge of possessiveness at the word "—drive to downtown Atlanta in the middle of the night in this weather. Particularly in that toy you call a car."

Catherine blinked. "What's wrong with my car?" The small red sports car was her one concession to frivolity, and she was mildly puzzled at his disparaging it.

"Absolutely nothing on short trips, during the day, and in good weather. But tonight there's the likelihood of flooding somewhere between here and the hospital. We'll take the Jeep," he said flatly, helping her into the vehicle.

Uneasiness at the thought of Catherine working out of a hospital located in one of the worst sections of Atlanta settled an ice-cold knot in his gut. Someone with her credentials should be affiliated with one of the many private medical centers found farther outside the city—away from danger. First chance he got, he intended to find out why she chose to practice there.

Next week he'd see about getting her something to drive that provided better protection, or at the very least, couldn't be blown away by the first stiff breeze.

His unexpected concern touched a place deep inside Catherine, creating a fragile hope—and the question whether she would ever fully understand this enigmatic man.

Mark didn't relax until Catherine finally emerged, several hours later, from behind the wide double doors marked Recovery. Her surgical scrubs, encasing her body from head to toe in wrinkled green cotton, were streaked with blood. She looked tired, he decided, but the earlier tension that had gripped her on the ride to the hospital was gone.

He waited for her to finish speaking with a nurse before rising from the uncomfortable plastic-covered couch and going to her. His arm automatically encircled her slender shoulders. "How was it?" For a split second she appeared startled to see him.

"Touch and go for a while," she said, her voice reflecting her fatigue, "but he's stable now."

"How was he hurt?"

Catherine flexed her shoulders, trying to ease the strain of the last several hours. "Knife fight, apparently. He got cut up pretty badly." She'd chosen to work at this hospital because she wanted to help those less fortunate than herself. But it was proving to be an impossible task. There was so much violence.

Mark studied the violet smudges under her eyes. She'd made the comments not expecting any reply. On impulse, he placed a quick kiss on her forehead.

"Do you need to stick around or can we get out of here?"

"I want to check him once more and get out of these." She indicated her stained clothing. "You know," she added almost as an afterthought, "he doesn't have any relatives. Just a foster family."

He didn't like her troubled look. Nor did he like the fact that she would again disappear behind those doors that effectively barred him from her. The thought was unsettling. "Take your time. I'll be right here."

She created a primitive need in him to protect her. And a violent urge to possess her that he found just short of terrifying.

Catherine was amazed how good—and right—it felt to find him waiting for her and to discuss the case with him. It still surprised her that Mark was genuinely interested in hearing about her practice.

As they were stepping off the garage elevator a short while later, a friendly voice hailed them from across the almost deserted parking deck. "Hey, Garrett."

Mark was immediately on guard as he turned to identify the caller. Catherine felt him stiffen slightly, his arm tightening around her. While his return greeting was friendly enough, Mark kept moving in the direction of the Jeep parked a few feet away.

A younger man, dressed in a police uniform, caught up with them. "What're you doing here at this hour? Don't tell me another one of your—"

"No," Mark interrupted. "One of my wife's patients had an emergency." He drew Catherine closer and made the necessary introductions.

Catherine noticed that Mark had deliberately cut the man off, but she was too exhausted to pursue it.

"When did you get married?" asked the obviously stunned officer, before remembering to offer his congratulations.

"A few hours ago. And," Mark added pointedly, "I'd like to get my bride home."

"Oh, right," the other man stammered. "Nice meeting you, Mrs. Gar— I mean Dr. Chambers. See you around, Garrett."

Something about the exchange troubled Catherine, but her tired brain wouldn't provide the key. Relegating the matter to a back corner of her mind, she gratefully sank into the passenger seat and let exhaustion claim her.

In the predawn light, Mark came awake fully aroused and acutely aware of Catherine lying against his side. Stroking a hand over her sleep-warmed body, he encountered the lacy blue bodysuit. When he'd put her to bed a few hours ago, exhausted and more than half asleep, he hadn't removed this last piece of clothing—in deference to her modesty. And his sanity.

As she stirred, subtly stretching into closer contact with his naked body, Mark conceded that the thin material was no barrier to his unrelenting desire for this woman who was now his wife. Cursing himself for not remembering how swiftly he could become sexually aroused in early morning, he began easing out of bed.

Catherine's arm tightened as he tried to pull away.

"Didn't mean to disturb you," he whispered huskily. "Go back to sleep."

Catherine slowly opened her eyes, but didn't relax her grip. "You must have put me to bed last night." There was a slight question in her tone—and mild embarrassment.

"No problem." The smile in Mark's voice became almost wicked. "It was my pleasure."

"Not the customary way to spend a wedding night," she observed, her own voice thick with sleep. "I don't think the bride is supposed to fall asleep as soon as she hits the bed." She hesitated. "Thank you."

"You mean you preferred it that way?"

"No." She raised her head so that she could see his eyes. "I'm thanking you for everything else you did for me last night." With deliberate intent, Catherine placed her lips against his.

Her genuine appreciation as much as the provocative gesture triggered Mark's tenuously leashed passion. In one smooth motion he tumbled Catherine onto her back, thrusting his tongue into her welcoming mouth.

She gloried in his frenzied reaction. This was what she wanted—to witness Mark lose his iron control.

Sensing the thin edge of his restraint, he dragged his mouth from hers. "If you're not going to sleep," he drawled, "I have an alternative suggestion."

"Yes." Her response was almost a demand.

His laugh was sensual. "Take this off," he ordered, the words raspy. "You've tantalized me with your body for weeks. Now I want to see it."

She felt the first stirrings of self-consciousness. Would he like what he saw? Well, she mocked herself, now was too late to worry. She fumbled with the tiny buttons running the length of the garment, but her nerveless fingers wouldn't cooperate.

Impatiently Mark brushed her hands aside but fared no better. Growling low in his throat, he grabbed a handful of the fragile material and ripped it from breast to crotch. A part of him was shocked at his action, but the sight of her drove the thought away.

Her nude body lying amid the ruins of her lingerie was exquisitely erotic, and the primitive part of him demanded that he take her at once. But another part counseled patience—advised him to take the time now to imprint himself on her.

But Catherine didn't allow him to slow down. She wanted his lovemaking fierce and unchecked. Wanted to know that, at least while absorbed in her body, he was completely hers. Sliding her fingers into his hair, she pulled his mouth back to hers.

Mark resisted her kiss with effort. "Easy, baby. We

have to slow down—" he laughed hoarsely "—or it's going to be over before it begins."

In guileless invitation, Catherine pressed her hips against his straining arousal.

"Sweetheart—" His voice held an edge of desperation as he fought to temper her as well as himself. He wanted time to explore her body, to bring her to the pinnacle of pleasure. "I can't—"

Her hips undulated against his, and she again sought his mouth, this time succeeding.

His capitulation came swiftly. "If this is the way you want it . . ." he managed to grate out, "you've got it."

Retaining enough sanity to wonder if she was ready to receive him, he frantically worked his hand down between them, all the while praying to some nameless god that once he'd had her—once he'd experienced all of her—this craving for her would diminish. Her moan of raw pleasure at his intimate touch told him she was as ready as he.

He entered her in one smooth stroke. She was wet and tight, and the feeling was unlike anything he'd ever experienced before.

Hot and fast . . . Thoughts careened through his brain in frantic phrases. *Too long . . . and I'll be consumed . . .*

The intense emotions roiling through Catherine were overpowering. The incredible feeling of oneness—of being connected more than just physically to Mark—took her by surprise. From somewhere deep inside an unfamiliar pressure began spiraling to urgent proportions, and she instinctively met him thrust for thrust.

In the headlong dash to completion, some inner voice again cautioned Mark to prolong their lovemaking. Through sheer willpower, he tried to slow them to a gentler rhythm. But it was too late. The explosion, when it came, was intense and satisfied much more than his physical craving. His own cry of release followed hers by only seconds.

Catherine was painfully aware of Mark's continued silence long after his breathing returned to normal. His body was rigid with tension. Though he held her firmly against his side, she was acutely aware that he'd distanced himself from her.

Their experience had been the most shattering of her life. She hadn't realized that making love could be like this—wild, yet so achingly tender. Inundated by all that he'd aroused in her, she hadn't questioned her own adequacy. Now, as he remained quiet, her self-doubt returned, and she wondered if he'd been disappointed.

Mark knew he was in deep trouble. The reality of sex with Catherine far surpassed the fantasy. *So much for useless prayers*, he thought cynically. He knew he should say something to her. But he was raw and vulnerable and feared that if he spoke to her just now, she would guess how fiercely she'd affected him.

Instead, he held Catherine tightly until she fell into an exhausted sleep.

SEVEN

Catherine finally gave up trying to elude the persistent light, carefully opening her eyes to locate the source of her torment. Early-afternoon sun spilled across the bed from the skylight above. Obviously, she concluded groggily, the room was not designed for late risers. As the fog of sleep lifted completely, she became acutely conscious of her surroundings, and that she was in bed. Alone.

Aching in places that brought warmth to her cheeks, she gingerly edged off the mattress and escaped to the bathroom. *Where was Mark?* Memories of her wanton abandon hours earlier appalled her, but that didn't prevent excitement from curling through her anew. Emotional control had always been the bedrock of her hard-won independence—control that seemed to be nonexistent where her new husband was concerned.

She stepped into the ceramic-tiled shower and under a steaming spray of water, hoping to dilute her thoughts. It gave her some comfort to recall that Mark's control had been, at best, tenuous. But even in his urgency, he had been an attentive and considerate lover. How did he rate her? She placed an unsteady hand on her stomach to still the quaver of apprehension.

Finishing her shower, she dressed quickly and went in search of Mark. She'd resolved to make the most of this marriage. If there were problems, she wouldn't discover them hiding in the bathroom.

But she didn't find him. Instead, in the kitchen, she found his terse note. *Have gone to get Beth. Back soon. M.* She reread the words several times as if some hidden message might appear. That he hadn't awakened her before he left troubled her, and she couldn't quell the small hurt caused by his silent departure.

Mark opened the door leading from the garage to the kitchen and stepped back, allowing Beth to enter ahead of him. *He was a coward.* He'd gone after her more for self-preservation than for the proper reasons—that he missed his daughter and wanted her with him and that Beth was anxious to see Catherine. No, his reason was much more basic than those. Beth was to be the buffer between himself and Catherine.

He'd hoped—prayed—that once having her, his desire for Catherine would become manageable. Unfortunately his initial instincts had been right—one time and he was addicted. There had been no pretense or artifice about her—traits common among the women he'd known previously. She might be cool, at times even remote, but while making love she'd been open and giving. And addicting.

Following Beth inside, he found the object of his troubling thoughts standing by the breakfast table, staring at his note. The rain had stopped shortly after dawn, and sunlight was streaming through the giant sliding-glass doors casting Catherine's features into stark relief.

Her wounded look disturbed him in ways he didn't want to analyze.

"CJ!" Beth ran straight to Catherine, wrapping her arms around her waist. "I missed you." Some of the child's innate shyness was still evident in the quiet words.

"And I missed you." Catherine hadn't realized until now just how much.

Mark studied the genuine pleasure replacing Catherine's previous expression as she enfolded his daughter and returned her hug. Against his will, the sincerity in the gesture began to thaw a part of him that had been frozen for as long as he could remember.

"Daddy said you guys are married."

As metal to magnet, Catherine's gaze was drawn to Mark. She wasn't prepared for the hint of vulnerability she glimpsed fleetingly in his eyes. It took a moment to compose herself enough to answer. "That's right, honey. Do you approve?"

"Oh, yes," Beth said, oblivious to the intense undercurrents eddying about her. As her initial shyness retreated, she caught hold of Catherine's hand. "Does this mean we can have a baby soon?"

"Well, I'm—" Catherine began.

But Mark cut her off. "Beth." His tone was mildly warning.

"Sorry, I just wondered." Disappointment tinged Beth's words, and she absently played with the ring on Catherine's left hand.

He felt a tiny pinch of envy that his daughter felt comfortable enough to ask that question of Catherine but not him. Hard on the heels of that thought came the unsettling realization that when he'd made love to Catherine in the dim predawn hours they'd failed to use any protection. The frantic pace of the last several days hadn't provided an opportunity for them to discuss birth control, and while he knew Catherine wanted a child—hell, wasn't that why she'd agreed to marry him?—it angered him that he'd forgotten something so fundamental.

"Did Daddy tell you he's going to let me take art lessons now?"

"No, he didn't." That Mark had relented and taken her advice touched Catherine deeply. Her gaze again sought his face only to find it now impassive. "I'm sure he was waiting for you to tell me. When do you start?"

"As soon as school is out."

"Good. That will give us plenty of time to get all the supplies you'll need."

Mark watched his daughter examine Catherine's wedding band. His wife hadn't given him a ring, and though he cursed himself for doing so, he couldn't help but wonder if this was another subtle sign of impermanence. In irritation he shook off the useless speculation. Survival dictated that a man learn from his mistakes, and he'd learned his lesson well. A man was a fool to trust a woman. If he hoped to protect himself, he knew he couldn't afford to listen to the tiny voice whispering that Catherine wasn't like the others.

"Daddy, when can I come to live with you and CJ?"

Her question was a pleasing surprise, while increasing his frustration another notch. "Soon, honey."

"Why not now?"

He sighed. "Because your grandmother wants you with her a while longer." He hated the half-lie, but he knew the truth might hurt his daughter.

"But I've lived with her forever." Beth's voice held a plaintive note.

"I know, honey. You just have to be patient a little longer," Mark told her gently.

With resignation Beth asked, "Do I have to go back tonight?"

"Punkin, you know you do. You have school tomorrow. But you'll be with us all next weekend."

Beth nodded somberly and sighed. "I guess that'll be all right."

Mark hugged her. "Be patient," he said again. "we're working on it."

It was another explicit reminder to Catherine of the real reason for their marriage.

"Why so pensive?"

Mark's words reached across the firelit room to where Catherine stood looking out a huge window that revealed nothing more to her than shadowy night images beyond. She rubbed her crossed arms. The rain of the night before had preceded an unseasonable cool front, and she welcomed the warmth of the fire.

"Beth didn't want to go back."

"No, she didn't," Mark agreed flatly.

"Why is she with Alice in the first place?" Catherine asked suddenly. She knew only the basic facts. Now she wanted details.

"Stupidity on my part."

Catherine looked at him with mild exasperation. "Could you be a bit more specific?"

Mark lurched out of his chair and began to prowl the room. "After Elise's death, Alice was simply . . . there and convenient." He sighed heavily. "In her own way she genuinely loves Beth, and I had to have someone competent to look after her while I worked. At first, I'd drop her off each morning and pick her up every evening. But as my work schedule became more and more demanding, I'd end up leaving Beth with her overnight.''

His words trailed off and Catherine waited for him to continue. ''And?'' she prompted.

''Finally she suggested that it would be simpler if I left Beth there during the week and saw her just on weekends.'' Mark ground his teeth, causing the muscles in his jaw to bunch. ''And that's where my stupidity comes in. I didn't see the pattern developing. For all intents and purposes, Alice had custody, and I appeared merely to have visitation rights.''

''This wasn't done by any legal means or procedure, was it?'' Catherine asked, her frustration once more surfacing.

''No,'' Mark assured her. ''But Beth has spent more time with Alice in her home than she's ever spent with me. The court won't ignore that. Particularly in a fight for permanent custody.''

Mark's voice took on a steely quality. ''Don't worry. We'll win this.''

Catherine roamed the room from one darkened window to the next, trying to work off her anger at the unfairness of the whole situation.

Mark dropped onto the sofa. ''Come sit down, Catherine.'' He patted the place beside him. ''We have to talk.''

She clearly heard his change in tone as well as topic. Again she felt faint apprehension. *Yes, I know.* Squaring her shoulders, she turned and walked over to him. He was slouched in his seat, his jeans-clad legs propped carelessly on the coffee table. She sat carefully on the edge of a cushion beside him and cleared her throat. The best way to get started on something unpleasant, she told herself firmly, was to plunge right in.

''I know I'm not a very good . . . lover.'' She

cleared the awkwardness from her throat. "But I'll be a . . . willing student." *Lord, talking about this was far worse than she'd imagined.* She kept her eyes trained on the fire dancing in the stone fireplace.

"What," Mark asked in measured words, "exactly are you suggesting?"

Catherine took in a lungful of air, hoping it would steady her voice and give her the courage needed to finish this conversation. "Just that I realize you may be disappointed in me—in my performance—when we make . . . love."

Mark studied her averted face in shocked silence. How could she possibly believe that after what happened between them in his bed early this morning? Hadn't it been blatantly evident just how desperately she'd made him want her?

"This is the second time you've suggested that you're somehow inadequate." He hadn't liked hearing it the first time. He liked it even less now.

Mark's words hardened into stones. "Tell me about the bastard."

The unexpected command startled her, and she relinquished, with reluctance, her inspection of the fire to look at him. "What?"

"I want to know why you keep putting yourself down." The tension slowly etching each of her features made him ache, but he would not back off this time.

The determined set of his jaw told her he wouldn't be dissuaded this time, and unease prickled down her spine. Her hands were clammy with nerves. But Mark did have a right, she supposed, to know where her hang-ups came from. She focused on her still-unfamiliar wedding ring, using it as a talisman.

"My mother deserted my father and me when I was very young. I don't really remember her, but I do remember my father was never happy after she left. He never adjusted. Over the years he became more and more withdrawn and bitter.'' Her thin smile felt brittle. "Apparently I'm a great deal like her, and my father decided he could punish me for her sins.''

A feral growl from Mark penetrated her protective cocoon, drawing her glance to his face. The anger engraved there stunned her. "Oh, it was never anything overt. He didn't physically abuse me, just made sure that nothing I did was ever good enough to please him.''

Leaving her seat, she wandered over to the fire and held out her hands as if trying to warm more than just her skin. "Initially I decided to go into medicine to please him. That proved to be the worst, and the best, decision I'd made up to that point in my life.''

God, he'd thought his own childhood was rough, but compared to Catherine's, his had been a picnic. At least his mother had made a clean break. She hadn't hung around making his life a living hell. His mouth twisted into a parody of a smile. "How can it be both.''

"Because of that decision, I met my ex-husband. Greg was a couple of years ahead of me in med school and not doing too well. Dad was on the faculty. What better way,'' Catherine asked in monotone, "for a failing med student to ensure passing grades than to marry the daughter of a key professor?''

The painful picture that was beginning to emerge tightened the knot in his belly. He wanted to stop her, but he somehow knew this needed to be said. He'd forced her to open this can of worms. The least he could do was to hear her out.

"But I really couldn't blame Greg.'' She laughed humorlessly at her own naiveté. "I was ripe for it. When he asked me to marry him, I thought it would change my life." Now that she had the momentum, she relentlessly plowed through the raw memories. "It did. But not for the better.

"I tutored Greg through his last two years of med school, and he passed. Just barely. As soon as he got his diploma, he informed me that our marriage was over."

Catherine paused, inwardly shuddering at the remembered hurt and humiliation. "He went on to tell me, quite explicitly, what a lousy lover I was and that I didn't have the ability to make a man happy. He certainly got no argument from me."

Her voice had dropped so low that Mark had difficulty hearing her. He unconsciously curled both hands into tight fists but said nothing, silently encouraging her to finish.

"As soon as he got his divorce from me, he married the woman he'd been having an affair with for the last year of our marriage."

"And he never knew about the baby?" Mark's words were amazingly gentle considering the fury raging inside him toward the bastard who'd been her husband.

She'd forgotten she'd told him that. Catherine shook her head. "No. He'd already left me by the time I discovered I was pregnant. I didn't want him back simply for the baby's sake." She shrugged in resignation, but her voice held a slight quiver. "It turned out to be a moot point anyway."

She was silent for several minutes until he asked softly, "And what's the best part of your decision?"

Her smile became almost serene. "By choosing surgery, I unwittingly provided my own salvation. My work is the one thing that's given satisfaction to my life."

He unfolded from his seat on the sofa and crossed the firelit space separating them.

He hadn't wanted Catherine to know just how fiercely she affected him. And having heard her story, he doubted she would ever guess. That might be fine for his peace of mind. But he could not allow Catherine to continue to believe herself somehow flawed—even at the risk of exposing his own vulnerable emotions.

Mark gently pulled her against his chest, easily subduing her weak struggles.

"You're the sexiest woman I've ever known," he breathed into her hair, holding her tight enough to keep her from escaping. "I get hard just looking at you." His voice was husky with sincerity. "And I can guarantee you're the best lay I've ever had."

Face flaming at his graphic words, Catherine pushed against his chest, trying to free herself. It wasn't the crudeness of the words that shocked her, but rather the compliment they contained. "I wasn't asking for compliments, Mark," she said with as much dignity as she could muster.

He refused to release her. "Oh, I'm certain of that." This woman had difficulty accepting even spontaneous ones. She sure as hell wouldn't ask for any. "After a few weeks of marriage to me, I have a feeling you won't question your desirability any longer. In fact," he said, running his hands over her back and finding immense satisfaction in her sensual shiver, "after tonight, you shouldn't have any doubts at all."

She was inordinately thankful that her face remained buried against his shoulder.

"But first we need to get back to what I originally wanted to talk with you about."

"You mean you didn't want . . .?" Catherine let her

voice dwindle away. *Nothing like jumping in with both feet.*

"To discuss your adequacy as a lover?" His smile was gentle. "No. However, it does have something to do with sex. Indirectly."

Catherine couldn't seem to assimilate the fact that he didn't find her lacking sexually and was having difficulty following the conversation. "What, then?"

"We've neglected to discuss the little matter of birth control."

Catherine's mind went blank, as if this were some totally foreign subject rather than one she discussed not infrequently in the course of her practice.

At her continued silence, he prodded, "You know, those magic devices that keep you from getting pregnant before you're ready?"

"Oh. Yes. Of course." She still felt off balance.

"Don't we need to decide who's responsible? What kind to use? If you're not already aware, I tend to get a bit . . . carried away during sex." *Particularly with you.* "And," he continued, his voice dropping to a suggestive whisper, "unless you want to get pregnant immediately, I need some answers before the next time."

Catherine cleared her throat, feeling absurdly disconcerted. "It's best not to use chemical methods if we . . . plan to have a baby soon." Somehow discussing contraception with Mark seemed as intimate as making love—more so, even.

Her mild embarrassment surprised him. He placed a hand on either side of her face so that she could no longer evade his eyes. "Are you asking me to take care of it?"

"Would you . . . mind?" she asked hesitantly. This

close his face seemed to encompass her whole world, his eyes to ask unspoken questions.

For a split second he wondered what it would be like to plan a pregnancy based on mutual love. The thought angered him.

"I'll take care of it. After all, that *is* my part in this bargain, isn't it? All you have to do is tell me when."

He couldn't understand why the idea of being used as a stud should bother him. It gave him what he wanted, didn't it? Access to Catherine's sexy body. And, he had to admit, simply being married to someone who *wanted* to have his child would be a refreshing change. But the empty feeling wouldn't go away.

Catherine jumped at the shrill ring of the telephone, and Mark released her to answer it. *Please, not tonight,* she silently prayed. She didn't think she could handle another emergency. She felt too raw, her emotions too chaotic.

But Mark wasn't handing her the phone. "Not tonight," he impatiently echoed her unspoken words into the receiver.

There was a brief pause.

"Who's involved?" Listening intently, he pushed one hand through his hair. "No." The word was without reservation. "You'll have to get Paul to handle it," he said with finality and directed a furtive look at Catherine. "Yeah, I'll check with you tomorrow. Thanks, Harold."

She watched him replace the receiver carefully, concerned by his troubled expression. "Problems?" Instinctively she reached out to him, and he drew her back against himself.

"Nothing that can't be handled for now by someone else," he prevaricated.

"Tonight I intend to show my wife just how desirable she is.'' Her fragility gave him the strength needed to temper his own desires. She needed tenderness, to be cosseted and soothed—things that had obviously been lacking in her life—not his unrestrained lust. He didn't stop to question the alien emotion driving him.

When he covered her mouth with his, the kiss was gentle but contained an underlying intensity. Catherine was powerless but to respond with the same intensity.

She couldn't remember how he managed, but somehow they were standing beside Mark's—their—huge bed. He quickly stripped off his own clothes, then undressed her with exquisite care. Gently placing her on the mattress, he followed her down.

"Last time I was in such a damned hurry I neglected to feel you . . . smell you . . . taste you. This time we'll go slow. I want you aching before we're done,'' he promised in a strained whisper. *That is, if I can hang onto my sanity.*

Catherine was overwhelmed by his loving. He was thorough and relentless and bound her to him in ways she could never hope to escape. The weight of his body possessing her was the only thing anchoring her to reality. When he'd driven her to the point of madness, when each sensual nerve ending was screaming for release, he kept her hovering on the brink for an excruciating eternity longer before finally allowing her to slip over the precipice into ecstasy.

Only then did he allow himself the same agony of pleasure.

Catherine protested weakly when he moved off of her. But he immediately pulled her against his side, and they slept.

Sometime during the wee hours, she was pulled from sleep fully aroused and ready for him. In explicit words he whispered his approval.

"It seems I've been hungry forever . . ." His husky voice sounded almost apologetic.

And again much later. "I can't seem to get enough . . ."

She eventually lost count of how many times he made love to her throughout the night, but with each successive loving he branded her in some unique way that slowly forged an unbreakable bond between them. Physically, at least, he didn't seem capable of keeping his distance.

By morning Catherine conceded that Mark had proven his point. He definitely found her desirable. And yet he'd remembered to protect her each time.

"Catherine," Mark called as he bounded up the stairs, his voice preceding him down the hall, "where are you?"

"In here," came her muffled response.

He found her in Beth's room up on a ladder fiddling with something on the top shelf of a bookcase. "What in hell are you doing up there?"

She spared him a quick glance and a smile. "I wanted to get the last of Beth's art supplies in place before she comes home this weekend."

His wife was wearing skintight pants covered by a floppy shirt. On the ground it would quite modestly cover her derrière. But up on the ladder, with her arms above her head, he was afforded an enticing view of her shapely behind—a behind she normally kept well hidden. He felt the familiar tightening low in his belly.

The outfit epitomized Catherine, he decided. On the outside she disguised her assets, but underneath she was sexy as hell. Surreptitiously she indulged what he was coming to learn was her true personality.

"How much longer will you be? I have something to show you, and if you stay up there much longer, it's not going to be what I originally planned," he added suggestively, feeling the pressure in his groin increase to an ache. He had to fight the urge to drag her down from that damned ladder, lay her on the rug, and possess her again—even though it had been mere hours since the last time. His growing obsession with her was expanding to uncontrollable proportions.

Okay, he conceded silently, *so he was obsessed with her body.* No big deal. He could handle that. There had to be other women who could do to his libido what Catherine did. Should the need ever arise, he'd find them. As long as he kept his heart intact, he was safe. Wasn't he?

"All finished." She held out a hand to him for assistance. Firmly grasping her by her slim waist, he effortlessly lifted her down from her perch.

Though he didn't release her immediately, Catherine could see that he'd distanced himself from her and wondered at the cause. "Thank you for allowing Beth to take art lessons. I promise you won't regret it."

Mark shrugged noncommittally. "No problem."

She sighed inwardly. "What was it you wanted to show me?"

"It's a surprise." Even white teeth flashed against Mark's deep tan as his face relaxed into a smile—something Catherine seldom saw. Today his smile was almost boyish. "Get your things and let's go."

Since their talk several nights ago, he felt compelled to find things to do for her. The vivid images her words had painted of a lonely childhood had affected him more than he liked to admit. He kept seeing her as a young girl reaching out and never receiving. Well, he could lavish her with gifts. But in a tiny corner of his heart, he conceded that material things didn't compensate for love.

Catherine didn't know where she expected him to take her, but a car dealership was not among her guesses. She looked questioningly at Mark as he escorted her out of his car and into the showroom. They weren't inside more than five minutes when she was introduced to the manager who directed them back outside and over to a bright red four-door Jeep Cherokee. He ceremoniously opened the door to the driver's side and handed her a set of keys.

"Mark?" she asked, her confusion evident.

"It's all yours, honey. Want to take it out and see what it can do?" he asked teasingly.

"Oh, Mark, this isn't necessary." His generosity was touching, but, knowing how mercenary his first wife had been, Catherine didn't want him to feel she also required material incentives.

Some of the genuine pleasure drained from his smile, and his voice hardened fractionally. "I think it is." He helped her into the driver's seat, then circled the van and climbed in.

"Do you have any idea what can happen to a woman stranded in the wrong place at the wrong time?"

His censure ignited her temper. "Yes," she snapped. "I *am* a doctor, and I've worked the emergency room."

"Well, honey, I've *seen* it happen," he stated succinctly. "I was too young to do anything about it the first time. Believe me, it's not a pretty sight." He visibly shuddered at the memory. "Eventually I learned how to defend myself and those around me."

Buying her a four-wheel-drive vehicle hadn't been a whim. He knew the area around County General Hospital well. And the thought of her being stranded in that section of town scared the hell out of him. He was well aware that the row upon row of tenement dwellings, scraped bare of all aesthetically pleasing qualities, spawned gratuitous violence. For the criminal element festering there, it was an invitation to exact retribution from anyone foolish enough to enter their domain. He knew firsthand what could happen to a woman alone in that situation.

The agony in his words squelched her anger and made her feel almost petty for not recognizing the significance of his gesture. "Mark, I'm sorry."

He brushed aside her sympathetic response, his voice now grim. "Can you drive a manual transmission?"

"Yes."

"Good. Do it."

She didn't argue.

"You need something that can withstand bad weather. The Jeep is heavy enough to get you through most minor flooding and any freak ice or snow we get around here."

She nodded.

"The heavily tinted windows will help keep anyone from knowing there's a woman driving alone. If you don't like this, we can get something else. But we will get something."

He'd obviously spent a great deal of time and consideration on this purchase. "Thank you, Mark," she said quietly. "This is perfect." His thoughtfulness nourished her fragile hopes.

But it was the fact that he'd chosen red that touched her most deeply.

EIGHT

"Hello, honey," Catherine greeted, collapsing into a chair at the patio table beside Beth, who was laboring over her drawing pad. Late-afternoon sunlight played hide-and-seek through the dense foliage surrounding the backyard, providing some relief from the sweltering June heat.

Catherine pulled the heavy French braid off her neck, savoring the cool breeze against her moist skin. After the harrowing day she'd had at the hospital, she was looking forward to simply absorbing the serenity. Mark had allocated very little formal lawn to the landscaping around the house, and most of the yard had been left in its natural state, requiring only minor maintenance. Twice each month he brought in several young people to do what yardwork and other odd jobs that were needed.

"Hi, CJ." Beth's response was gloomy.

"What are you working on?"

"I'm trying to finish this stupid picture for art class."

Catherine fought to conceal a smile. "Is this the

same art class you were raving about only a couple of weeks ago?''

''Well, yes,'' she conceded sheepishly, ''but I can't get this right. Can you help me?''

Diverting her attention from the impromptu game of touch football in progress on the minuscule lawn between Mark and an assortment of teenagers who worked for him, Catherine examined Beth's charcoal sketch. ''I'm afraid I wouldn't be much help, honey. I can't draw a straight line with a ruler.''

Beth sighed in frustration.

''I have an idea,'' Catherine said with sudden inspiration. Maybe Beth was the key to the vague plan that had been floating around inside her head. ''Why don't you ask your dad to help?''

''You think so?''

''Here he comes now,'' Catherine said as Mark, followed by his young teammates, climbed the deck stairs. He was wiping perspiration from his face with a towel. Watching the ripple of chest muscles beneath his damp, grass-stained T-shirt set off the customary frisson of awareness low in her pelvis, making it difficult to concentrate. ''Ask him.''

As if attuned to her reaction, his eyes locked with hers in sensual promise. Holding the connection, he sent the rest of the group indoors for soft drinks and to wash up before focusing his attention to Beth. ''Ask me what?''

''I can't get this picture to turn out right. Will you help me?''

Mark looked as if he was going to refuse. Sensing his inner conflict, Catherine held her breath. After a moment he dropped resignedly into the chair on the other side of Beth.

''Let's see what you've got.'' He studied the paper

and listened to Beth explain what the teacher had asked them to do. After a minute he picked up the charcoal and with concise, efficient movements began to draw.

As he became absorbed in the project, Catherine watched in satisfaction as his features relaxed into pleasure.

"Daddy, that's perfect!" Beth exclaimed when he'd produced the desired effect.

Mark handed the charcoal back to her. "Now you do it." He turned over a clean sheet of paper and waited patiently while she followed his example.

Once she'd successfully completed the exercise, Beth threw her arms around his neck. "I did it! Thanks for your help, Daddy."

Mark closed his eyes, savoring the feel of one of the increasingly spontaneous hugs from his daughter.

When Mark's gaze connected with Catherine's, the naked gratitude she saw brought a lump to her throat. Struggling to control the fullness in her chest, she picked up the sketch pad and flipped back to his drawing. *He does have talent*, she thought almost triumphantly.

During their brief marriage, Catherine had witnessed Mark deny his own talents on more than one occasion. He deferred to a team of architects, but when design problems arose, he was the one who frequently came up with the needed modifications. Though he tried to hide it, his frustration was palpable at times. She was determined to get him to acknowledge his talent and experience the pleasure of allowing himself to do what he loved.

"Hey, Garrett," a street-wise youth Catherine had gotten to know as Tiger shouted from the house, "you're wanted on the phone."

There was something special between Mark and these kids. It went beyond an employer/employee relationship. Catherine wished Mark would share whatever it was with her.

"Be right there." Mark reluctantly released Beth and went inside to take the call.

Minutes later, he came to the patio door. "I've got to go out for a while." He was dragging on a clean shirt, carelessly tucking it into tight-fitting jeans.

Catherine felt her stomach tighten. This was what? the fourth or fifth time in the few weeks they'd been married that Mark had received one of these mysterious calls. "Do you know how long you'll be gone?" She hoped he couldn't detect her anxiety.

A muscle flexed along his jaw. "No." He came over to where she sat, pulled her roughly into his arms, and covered her mouth with a hard kiss. "I'll be back." It sounded like a vow. "Don't hold supper and don't wait up," he said flatly and strode back inside to round up the others.

The first time a call had come, Catherine thought little of it. Anyone running his own business got calls at odd hours. In fact, Mark had passed it off as work-related problems. But a pattern had begun to develop— one that had ominous undertones. A call would come, and Mark would leave and be gone anywhere from an hour to half the night. After some of them, he came home looking haggard. But what made her most uneasy was the fact that there was never any plausible explanation forthcoming.

And no matter how hard she tried, she couldn't allay her silent questions.

It was late when Mark returned, but Catherine was awake. As always when he was away, she'd been unable to sleep.

There was no moon tonight—nothing, save some

slight radiated light, to penetrate the unrelenting darkness. She heard him undress and go into the master bath to shower.

A short while later, he eased himself into bed and reached for her. She went willingly into his arms.

"Are you all right?" she whispered in the darkness.

She wished she felt secure enough to question him. She wished he trusted her enough to confide in her. But he had been very explicit that each of them was to retain autonomy in this marriage—and she had accepted that. She feared the consequences if she were to push the issue.

"I need you." His voice was husky with arousal and something else she couldn't fathom. "Let me inside you and I'll be fine." He covered her mouth with his, the fine tension in his body communicating itself to hers.

The ache came sharp and sweet—her love for this man all mixed up with the wanting. If it was her body that held him to her, she would give him something worth remembering.

Breaking the kiss, she raised up on one elbow so that she was partially draped over him. "You know, you've never given me the chance to make love to *you*." Her laugh was seductive. "You always seem to have me flat on my back before I can think twice."

His chest lifted on a sensual chuckle. "Your fault for always making me want to do outrageous things to you."

She leaned down to tease his mouth with hers, not quite touching but tantalizing him until he groaned low in his throat. He smelled of clean soap, and the thought came unexpectedly that she resented that—it obliterated Mark's unique, musky scent.

He groaned again in warning. "Are you sure you know what you're inviting?"

"Lie back and let me love you." Her use of the word was deliberate, even though he wasn't to know that. She might not be able to tell him she loved him in words, but she could tell him with her body.

Getting to her knees beside him, she smoothed her hands over his torso, and he fell silent except for his labored breathing. She touched her mouth to skin that felt like shorn velvet underlaid with granite-hard muscle, exploring a path down his chest to his firm, quivering stomach.

Some primitive instinct was guiding her, and, with slow, lingering kisses and sure fingers, she moved lower. Taking him into her mouth, she urged him to the brink.

He chanted her name incoherently, clutching the sheets as if they were the only stable thing in his universe and trying to hang onto what control he had left. He needed her sweetness, he acknowledged with undiluted honesty, probably always had. With his last ounce of willpower, he tried to pull Catherine beneath him.

But she evaded him, straddling his hips instead.

"Protection?" he asked, his voice guttural.

With a sophistication born of the moment, she reached for the small foil packet and made the procedure an erotic torment. When the task was completed, she took him inside herself as he'd asked her an eon ago and set the pace in rhythm with the need driving him.

"God . . . Catherine, I—" He bit off what he was about to say as his body—and his soul—erupted with emotions so exquisite they bordered on pain.

Catherine sensed a desperation about him tonight, as if their lovemaking might cleanse him. But she couldn't keep her thoughts from scattering in the wake of her own devastating climax.

Mark tucked one arm behind his head and stared out the window at the dawn painting the night sky in hues of pink and orange. His other arm held Catherine securely against his side.

Knowing how uncertain she was about her own sensuality, that she had made such overwhelmingly beautiful love to him touched a part of him he thought was untouchable. His response to what she had done to him, what had happened between them, confirmed how vulnerable he'd become to her.

He'd suspected he was in deeper than he proclaimed even to himself—definitely more than was wise if he hoped to protect himself. She got through all his defenses much too easily. Hell, he was *already* addicted to her. He might not believe in love but . . . He shied away from completing the thought.

It was bad enough that he'd come to crave her physically. But love? No, not in this lifetime. She merely fulfilled certain basic needs, he tried to tell himself. But the uneasy premonition assailing him did nothing for his peace of mind.

He didn't want Catherine getting the wrong idea about their lovemaking. He feared that sometime, when he was defenseless against her all-consuming passion, he might inadvertently blurt out the wrong words—words that he wouldn't mean. Words that would later have to be retracted. And a part of him couldn't bear the thought of how that might hurt her.

Above all he owed her—and himself—honesty. He'd take care of it in the morning.

"Good morning," Catherine murmured, coming up

behind Mark where he stood at the kitchen counter and sliding her arms around his waist. She felt the subtle tensing of his muscles, not in anticipation but in self-defense.

"Morning." He took his time pouring his coffee. "Want a cup?"

Catherine stepped away from him. "Thank you, I'll get my own," she said, holding her tone neutral, and busied herself with the task.

She should have guessed this would happen when she again awakened to an empty bed. It was always the same. At night they made soul-shattering love, but during the day Mark withdrew into himself, placing an invisible barrier between them. She'd hoped this time might be different.

It was painful to admit that her hopes were apparently futile.

"Look, Catherine—" Mark forked the fingers of one hand through his already ruffled hair.

Turning to face him squarely, she leaned against the counter, lifted her chin, and took an unwanted sip of coffee. "Yes, Mark?"

"About last night . . ." The bruised look on Catherine's face cut into him. *Get on with it, Garrett.*

She held his gaze steadily. "What about it?"

He muttered a succinct expletive under his breath. He hadn't envisioned honesty being this difficult.

"What I feel for you—what we feel together—is lust. Pure and simple. Don't make it into something it's not."

Well, this wasn't exactly what she'd expected. But on the other hand it wasn't unexpected, either. She willed herself not to react. "Is there a particular reason for telling me this?"

He studied her now-expressionless face. "We're

pretty potent in bed together.'' Damn, was *that* an understatement. ''I wouldn't want you to misinterpret anything that might be said in the heat of the moment.''

''Such as?''

''Men have been known to tell a woman he loves her when what he really means is that he wants her like hell.'' God, he hated spelling it out.

Bracing herself, she asked, ''And would that be so terrible?''

Yes! he wanted to shout. He wouldn't—couldn't—give her that weapon.

''Damn it, Catherine, don't complicate things between us. What we have is . . . At least it's honest.'' Something raw flickered in his eyes, then was gone. ''And honesty's the one sure thing we have going for us.''

She ignored the pain lashing her. If his feelings for her were as basic as he wanted her to believe, why bother with this little speech? *Because Mark has a strong sense of right and wrong,* Catherine answered her own question.

He'd made his position on love painstakingly clear before they married. But if he could so easily control his feelings, mocked a little voice in her head, what kept him from eventually controlling his physical need of her? She sensed an underlying vulnerability in Mark—a fear of committing too much of himself—and despaired of ever discovering the cause.

The only thing holding her panic at bay was the thought that he still needed her for Beth and the custody suit. But how much time did that give her?

''All right, Mark. We'll play it your way.'' She looked at her watch, her smile seemingly unperturbed. ''I've got to get to the hospital.''

NINE

He should tell Catherine.

Mark braked sharply, cursing under his breath at a noonday jaywalker's disregard for personal safety. Keeping this from her, he told himself grimly, wasn't fair. She had a right to know. Wasn't *he* the one who placed such a high premium on honesty—even at the cost of hurting Catherine on more than one occasion?

Furious would be too mild a description for his own reaction should he suddenly discover his wife was deliberately placing herself at risk, particularly if he hadn't been aware of it. The latest encounter had been too close for even *his* comfort. For the second time in less than a month he'd nearly ended up in the middle of a drug war shootout while attempting to keep "his" kids out of the backlash.

Mark shuddered recalling the events of only a few days ago. This time Tiger had been involved and headed for trouble. Mark had finally located the kid in a burned-out tenement, caught between two gangs embroiled in a deadly altercation over drugs and turf.

It had quickly escalated into gunfire. Grabbing Tiger by the arm, Mark began inching their way to safety.

"Hey, man, where're you taking me?"

"I'm getting you—and me—the hell out of here! In case you haven't noticed, those are real bullets they're firing!"

Tiger jerked against Mark's death grip on his arm. "I can't leave my buddies, man! They need me."

"You won't be any use to them dead," Mark growled, alternately crawling and crouching behind whatever cover was available, dragging a resisting Tiger behind him.

The kid reminded him too much of himself at that age, before Joe came along. Reckless and obstinate. Except Mark had a sick feeling in his gut that he wasn't going to be able to save this one from himself.

Another round of gunfire and a scream told Mark that someone had been hit. The wail of sirens sent the gang members scattering—all except the unfortunate kid who was down and probably dying . . . or already dead.

Tiger again wrenched against Mark's hold. "Hey, that's Tony! He's my friend. I gotta go help him!"

"Your 'friend' is a damned drug dealer. If you think I'm going to let you risk your life on that trash, you're crazy. The police will handle this." Mark didn't relinquish his hold on Tiger. "We're getting the hell out of here."

The blare of a car horn jolted Mark back to the present. He'd somehow managed to get Tiger away from there last night. But he knew the kid wasn't out of danger. The same scenario was destined to happen over and over. And sooner or later, Tiger would be pulled into the carnage and irreparably harmed.

Mark didn't want Catherine involved in this. That

was why he still hadn't told her about his work with street kids. There was something untouched, uncontaminated, about her that he didn't want to tarnish with this ugliness. He didn't want her subjected to the sordid side of life that he'd grown up in—that he still saw too frequently.

That was part of it, he conceded as he eased the pickup ahead in the bumper-to-bumper traffic, but not the only reason. Years of harsh experience had taught him that if he trusted too much—if he revealed too much—the knowledge could be devastating in the wrong hands. Especially a woman's.

He had a theory about women. They weren't to be trusted. Ever. They always had an angle, and they always wanted something. He'd had ample experience, and he'd never met an exception. Whether his inadequate mother who'd deserted him, his unfaithful exwife who'd threatened to abort his child, or his devious mother-in-law who'd talked him into letting her care for Beth and was now trying to take her away from him, every female who had played more than a casual role in his life had ultimately betrayed him.

But something about Catherine made his theory ring false. Still, he reminded himself, even she wanted something from him. A child.

He pulled into the underground parking space reserved for Paul Martin's clients, right next to Catherine's red Jeep. No, he wasn't ready just yet to tell her everything. He'd tell her some things. In fact, it surprised him how easy it was to tell her most things. But a few he kept to himself. Those that made him most vulnerable.

And this was one. He didn't want her knowing exactly what he did for these kids. Or how important helping them was to him. That would be revealing a part of himself he wasn't yet ready to expose.

"Have a seat," a somewhat harassed Paul offered, ushering Catherine into his office. "I'm amazed you could get away from the hospital so quickly."

"Your message sounded urgent." Concluding that the chairs, in addition to other assorted furniture, must have been provided for the sole purpose of holding the mountains of law books and manila folders populating every available surface, she chose one with the least amount of clutter and cleared a place to sit. "Where's Mark?"

"He'll be along shortly. He had to take care of a problem."

"Anything serious?" His offhand remark triggered the doubts that recently had begun to buzz just beneath her facade of self-confidence.

"No. It shouldn't take long," he said off-handedly. "You don't mind if we wait until he arrives before discussing my news, do you?"

"No." What else could she say?

Smiling, Paul pinned her with an astute stare. "How's married life?"

Paul, she decided, was almost as direct as Mark and every bit as clever at changing the subject. Leaving her seat, she went to gaze out at the Atlanta skyline.

"No complaints." *Except that I don't know where my husband goes from time to time.* "A few questions maybe."

"Oh?" Catherine sensed Paul's defenses being activated. "Questions?"

"Tell me about the kids he has working for him."

"What do you want to know?"

She turned away from the view of downtown to face

him, leaning back against the wide sill. "Who are they? Where do they come from?"

"From the housing projects mostly. All of them are disadvantaged in some way."

His answer wasn't exactly evasive, but for the most part she already knew all that. "Why?" she persisted.

"Why does he hire them?"

She nodded.

"To do light work around the sites." He was choosing his words carefully now. "It's good experience for them, not to mention good training. Why do you ask?" He turned the question back on her.

It couldn't be clearer that he intended giving her no new information. She sighed inwardly. "No reason. I just wondered."

"Give it time, Catherine," he said quietly. "I warned you he wasn't easy to understand."

"I just hadn't realized to what extent. Or how much time it might take."

His face relaxed into a smile again. "As long as we're waiting," he said, shuffling through a pile of papers on his desk, "there are a couple of things I need to go over with you. The taxes are due on that house you own. Do you plan to sell, or should I pass the bill on to the accountant?"

Even though she'd asked Paul to handle her business affairs, and welcomed his input, his question startled her. Her small home, purchased shortly after finishing her surgical residency, had been her first act of independence. True, she'd spent a great deal of time and effort fixing it up, but it represented more than a personal possession. It had become a symbol of sorts of her own self-sufficiency. Though she hadn't given the house much thought lately, she certainly hadn't considered selling it.

"Is there a reason I should?"

"None. Except that you don't need it." He looked at her shrewdly. "Do you?"

"All the same," she said, unsure why she was being noncommittal, "I think I'll hang onto it for a while. Give me the bill, and I'll take care of it."

A faint rustle prompted Catherine to look toward the doorway. Mark stood framed in the opening. He'd obviously come straight from the job site, but even in jeans and gray chambray shirt, he commanded attention. Familiar heat curled through her.

For a microsecond a nerve rippled at his jaw, then stilled. "Send the bill to my accountant, Paul," he ordered softly, crossing the room to Catherine.

She wanted to object to his high-handedness but, trapped in his glittering stare, thought better of it. She'd straighten it out at some later date, she told herself as she warily tracked his progress toward her.

Stopping in front of her, Mark placed both hands on her shoulders, as if to keep her from bolting. "Hello . . . wife," he said huskily just before covering her mouth with a kiss that conveyed some tightly leashed emotion.

The fact that another person was in the room didn't register. Catherine simply clung to him, allowing her body to lean into his, giving in to the powerful effect Mark had on her.

"Okay, you two, cut it out," Paul complained good-naturedly, "you're embarrassing me."

Mark slowly lifted his head, noting with primitive satisfaction Catherine's flushed features, before directing a mock scowl at Paul. "That'll be the day."

"Everything squared away?" Paul asked him.

"Yeah."

"Good." An indecipherable look passed between the two men. "Have a seat. I've got some good news."

"That's a switch," Mark muttered, guiding Catherine back to her seat. He emptied another chair of legal documents and placed it within touching distance of hers. "Let's have it."

"Alice has withdrawn her custody suit."

Paul's words created conflicting feelings in Catherine—elation that Mark's ordeal was at last over, followed by a bone-chilling dread of the effect this would have on Mark's and her fragile relationship.

He leaned forward in his chair. "Why?" There was no inflection in the word, but it held a wealth of suspicion.

Paul shook his head in exasperation. "Just once can't you accept something at face value?"

"Not this," he stated unequivocally. "After months of her making our lives hell, it doesn't make sense."

"Her attorney says Alice is, uh, impressed—his word, not mine—with how well Beth's done since your marriage. That, and the fact she realizes how badly Beth wants to come and live with you," Paul added. "Says she doesn't want to upset the child any further."

Mark made a scoffing sound, his expression now skeptical.

"Bottom line is that her attorney probably told her she didn't have much chance of success. Not after the psychologist's positive report on you two and Beth."

Mark surveyed his friend with keen perception. "Let's have the rest of it."

"Right." Paul sighed. "She wants reasonable visitation rights. If you don't oppose her on this, she'll legally relinquish any rights she might have to raise the custody issue again."

Pinching the bridge of his nose, Mark squeezed his

eyes shut. God, he wanted to say no. Wanted to shout it. But he wouldn't. Beth cared for her grandmother, and for that reason, and that reason alone, he told himself, he wouldn't challenge her. "Agreed." The word was low and gravelly.

Catherine didn't miss Mark's thinly veiled aversion and knew, without his having to tell her, what it cost him not to refuse. She wasn't certain she could have been as generous.

"Good decision," Paul commended. "We'll petition the court for a binding custody decree. Merely a formality, but that will make everything official and any future claims more difficult."

"Make it ironclad." Mark's tone was uncompromising.

"I'll do my best."

"How soon can we get Beth?"

"Alice asked to keep her until Saturday." Paul looked questioningly at his friend. "That okay?"

"Only if that's the best we can do." Mark unfolded from his chair and extended his right hand, offering a firm handshake. "Thanks, Paul."

Mark's silver-gray gaze again fastened on Catherine. "Do you have to get back to the hospital?"

It was the first indication since Paul had disclosed his news that Mark remembered she was even in the same room. "No, I'm finished for the day."

"Care to take a ride with me?" He reached for her hand. "There's something I want to show you."

The hint of a smile warmed his slate-gray eyes. But the slight tremor in the strong fingers closing around hers told Catherine that he'd been more affected by the last few minutes than his demeanor would suggest. She wondered, with an odd foreboding, if her purpose in his life had now been served.

*   *   *

"Oh, Mark, it's beautiful." Inhaling deeply from her climb to the top of Stone Mountain, Catherine took in the sweeping view. The huge hunk of granite rose out of the earth like a misshapen crown offering a unique exposure to the hazy Georgia landscape for miles in all directions. "It almost takes my breath away."

Mark laughed softly, watching the rapid rise and fall of her breasts. "It does do that." He'd been surprised—and pleased—when she opted for the forty-five-minute hike rather than taking a cable car. "But it's worth it."

The reverent note that had entered his voice pulled her gaze to his face. He looked as relaxed—and open—as she'd ever seen him. "I've been to the park many times but never made it to the top of the mountain. Do you come up here often?"

Mark dropped onto an outcropping of rock, propping his forearms on his bent knees, and studied the spectacular view. Joe had introduced him to what Mark had come to consider his own private retreat shortly after they'd met. This was the first time he'd ever wanted to share it with someone. "Yeah, whenever I can."

Finding a spot nearby, Catherine followed suit. "Other than the obvious, what makes it special?"

He shrugged. "I guess because it's so different from where I grew up. There's a sense of freedom up here, and serenity." His smile became self-mocking. "There're no boundaries except those we impose on ourselves," he added, indicating the protective fencing that ringed the top of the mountain.

"Tell me about where you grew up."

He'd given her the barebone facts, but he knew she was asking for specifics. He'd once told her, an eon ago, that if she wanted to know something about him she had to ask. Well, now she had. "There's not much worth mentioning about inner-city slums. They're dirty, concrete prisons inhabited by too much garbage—the human variety as well as the inanimate kind."

She shivered in the hot July sun. "How were you able to survive alone?"

"When your life's on the line, it's amazing how quickly you learn." He picked up a small chunk of granite, his fingers caressing its irregular surface. "There's a kind of underground network on the streets. Once you find your niche, you can get almost anything—for a price." He tossed the stone harmlessly away. "Survival boils down to learning how to negotiate the lowest personal cost for what you need."

Some innate sense told her he wasn't talking about money, but what was expected in return for whatever commodity—necessary or otherwise—was sought. The pain that scenario spawned in her was almost unbearable.

"Is that how you got the scar on your cheek?" She wanted to reach out and touch it, but she didn't.

"Yeah," Mark said, unconsciously stroking the old wound with one finger. "I guess it is. The leader of a local street gang bet me I couldn't hold my own for five minutes in a knife fight in a dead-end alley. I needed money for food, so I took him on."

"My God." Catherine felt terror as tangible as if the scene were presently unfolding before her. "How old were you?"

He shrugged. "I don't remember. Fifteen, sixteen, maybe. I was big for my age."

When it appeared he wasn't going to continue, she prompted, "Finish the story. What happened?"

"I won." He didn't tell her that the victory had come with its own price. The reputation of being mean with a knife had followed him until Joe came along.

"You got cut!" she said in contradiction to his blasé attitude. "The lesion wasn't properly tended."

Mark nodded his head in confirmation. "A guy in the projects who was good with a needle took care of it."

The unspoken details made her cringe. "Why didn't you go to the county hospital? That's what it's there for."

"Couldn't risk it. I was underage, and they would've called in the authorities."

"Surely there were agencies that could have helped?"

"None that I wanted to have anything to do with. I had no intention of being shuffled from one foster home to another," he stated grimly. "Eventually I had to learn to take care of myself. I simply did it a little sooner than most. I was fortunate really. I was able to keep from selling my body and I managed to avoid the drug scene. About the worst thing I had to do was sell my blood." He rolled his shoulders in fatalistic acceptance. "It wasn't so bad."

And hell is a tiny bit too warm. "Tell me about Joe." It gave her some measure of comfort knowing that Mark's life had improved once Joe entered it.

His expression softened with memories. "He had an effective way of making a smartass listen to reason. Wouldn't tolerate excuses or backtalk, and damn, could he make you toe the line." Mark chuckled, recalling the scuffles between the two of them before he'd finally learned it was easier—and smarter—to listen than to fight.

"What was he like?"

Mark gave her question careful consideration before answering. "Joe was one of those rare people who tries to do something to make this world a better place rather than just talking about it. And he believed that you always repay what you've received.'' Mark stopped abruptly.

There was more that could be said here, Catherine realized, but it was obvious he wasn't going to elaborate.

Instead, he said, "He seemed to think there was something worth salvaging in me. God only knows what."

"I don't imagine it was all that hard to find." The soft comment was out before Catherine thought about it.

The pleasure her spontaneous remark created in him was unsettling. He ran his eyes over her flushed features, noting the way the wind had loosened her dark hair from its French braid. "Don't you?" He smiled crookedly, tucking a wayward strand behind one ear when what he really wanted to do was free it from its restraints and bury his hands in its silkiness.

As he studied her, Catherine detected some elemental conflict fleetingly mirrored in his eyes and then obliterated.

"Thank you." His voice sounded strained.

Confused, she asked, "For what?"

"For giving me back my daughter."

Though she'd love to take credit for that, her honesty wouldn't allow it. "Mark, with or without me, you would have worked out your problems with Beth. She loves you very much."

"Maybe." He didn't sound convinced. "The court might not have been as understanding. Either way, I appreciate what you've done."

His gratitude, while sincere, was offered as if it were a debt which must be paid. And he was a man who always paid his debts, she thought, her doubts again surfacing. Clearing a lump from her throat, she returned to their former topic. "What did you learn from Joe?"

He let his gaze travel out as far as the horizon would allow. "That there was more to survival than fighting with my fists—or knives. He showed me how to channel my antagonism toward the world into something creative. Garrett Construction is the result." Surging to his feet, he strode the short distance to the chain-link fence. "He was with me through the lean years. He should have lived long enough to reap the benefits. God, I miss him."

She watched the muscles of his broad back flex beneath his workshirt and felt the agony of caring in his words. She was beginning to realize that when Mark allowed himself to care, it ran deep, and she yearned to be the recipient of his caring. Aching with him, she wanted to go to him but wasn't certain he would appreciate her intrusion.

After several minutes, he expelled a deep breath. "We need to get back," he said, coming to stand in front of her. "I need to check something at the construction site before I take you to pick up your car."

She looked up at him wryly, feeling the stiffness in her legs from the unaccustomed climb. "Fine, if I can get my body to cooperate."

Mark hunkered down beside Catherine and, starting with her tender calves, began to knead the tight muscles through the thin fabric of her slacks. He was incredibly gentle, she marveled, for such a hard man. As his warm, strong hands massaged their way up her legs, the heat he was now generating was of a distinctly different nature, pooling in the sensitive area between her thighs.

It never ceased to amaze her how effortlessly Mark could reduce her to a mass of quivering need. She groaned softly, not certain whether from the easing of her muscle spasms or from the erotic stimulation of his hands. At the sybaritic sound, Mark's gaze streaked to hers, his eyes already dilated to almost black.

"You always make me ache."

Her frank remark did things to him. With one strong hand he cupped her intimately.

At his touch, her breath hissed through her teeth.

Abandoning her leg, he captured her right hand and pressed it against the rigid bulge straining the fly of his jeans. "You should know by now that the ache is mutual." His voice was hoarse, his own breathing erratic.

Abruptly he withdrew his hands and quickly helped her to her feet. "We better get the hell out of here before I do something that'll not only embarrass us both but is guaranteed to get us arrested." The relaxed mood was gone, replaced by the renewed sexual tension that simmered between them.

During the drive, Catherine rested her head against the seatback, trying to cool the hot desire raging within her by pondering their conversation. It helped strengthen her fragile hope that perhaps she was coming to understand him better. This was the most candid Mark had been about himself. Some of the things he'd talked about had been almost too painful to hear. And she knew instinctively that he still held things back. But it was a beginning, wasn't it? There'd been a closeness between them this afternoon that she hadn't experienced before. That had to count for something.

Mark pulled his concentration away from the road long enough to glance at Catherine. Her eyes were closed, but he couldn't tell if she was asleep. He supposed he could attribute his uncharacteristic talkativeness to the euphoria of having learned that he wasn't going to lose Beth. Still, he was astounded at how much he'd told her during the course of the afternoon.

He'd never divulged this much to anyone, let alone a woman. Particularly a woman who periodically gave subtle indications that maybe their relationship wasn't permanent. Learning that she intended to hang onto her house was the latest. Why? That she'd never answered Paul's question bothered him. He knew he could ask her outright, and she'd give him an honest answer. But he didn't want to have to ask. For some reason he couldn't explain, he wanted her to volunteer the information.

Swinging the pickup into the site entrance, he pushed his brooding thoughts aside. As soon as he shut off the engine, Catherine opened her eyes and smiled at him. He loved her like this—all soft and vulnerable, with her guard down. It brought out his protective instincts. It also made him horny as hell.

To break the spell he asked, "You want to wait in the truck? I won't be long."

Catherine straightened in her seat. "No, I'd like to go in with you, if you don't mind. I like seeing you at work."

He wasn't sure he could concentrate with her inside the close confines of the trailer distracting him. "Let's go then." Mark got out of the truck and came around to help her down. "I don't want to be here all night."

On the one hand, he was secretly pleased that she was interested in his work. On the other, it irritated him like hell. He couldn't shake the feeling that she perceived far more about him than he wanted. She threatened his battered heart on a level he'd never come close to experiencing before.

Once inside the trailer, he took down a thick roll of blueprints and spread them across a large table at one end of the room. He studied several sheets closely, busily scratching figures on a pad.

"What are you working on?"

"There's a problem integrating the cooling system on top of the building so that it doesn't detract from the architectural design."

"Oh." It sounded complicated, but she'd learned during her short marriage that her husband absorbed information like a sponge. He listened and learned from the people who worked for him. His greatest love was designing buildings, though he continued to deny himself that pleasure. When his architects went over the blueprints with him, he seemed to itch to get his hands on the plans. But he only intervened in a crisis when no one else seemed capable of finding a solution.

He completed several more rather involved computations, then took out another sheet of paper and quickly sketched a design. "I think that'll do it. I'll leave it here for the crew to go over in the morning."

The whole procedure hadn't taken Mark that long. Yet she knew that the problem had been plaguing the crew for some time. "If it's this easy for you to figure out the mistakes in someone else's work, why aren't you doing the work to begin with?" she asked.

Mark looked up from his notations to stare at her. "Because I'm not a designer. I told you that."

"Why?"

"Why what?" he asked warily as he marked the blueprint pages and took them, along with his notes, to the desk.

"Why aren't you the designer?"

He turned to face her, spreading his booted feet wide and folding his arms across his chest. "We've been over this before."

But this time she wasn't going to back off. "Was Joe aware of your ability?"

"Drop it, Catherine." His combative stance told her she'd struck a nerve.

"He must have known," she guessed intuitively. "From what you've told me about Joe, I'll bet he thought it a terrible waste not to use all your talents to their fullest extent."

Mark winced slightly but didn't comment. She'd nailed that right on. Joe had wanted him to develop his talent for design. He'd begged Mark to study architecture. In fact, it was the one area in which he had disappointed the older man.

"One more thing and then I'll drop it," she said quietly, holding his warning glance. "Just for the record, I agree with him."

Mark was amazed at how much her words stung. Just one more indication, he thought cynically, of how far she'd gotten under his defenses. When the phone at his elbow rang, he snatched it up before it completed the cycle.

"So talk," he snapped into the receiver.

Catherine didn't have to hear a single word on the other end to know what the conversation was about. Mark's now-closed expression said it all.

Silently leaving the trailer, she went to wait in the truck.

He joined her a short while later but said nothing, simply starting the engine and heading in the direction of her Jeep.

Finally Catherine broke the silence. "Don't tell me, let me guess. You've got to go out. You don't know for how long, but I shouldn't hold supper and I shouldn't wait up." She turned slightly in her seat to face him. "Right?"

His silver eyes cut to hers, but she could barely make out his features in the waning light of dusk. "That about covers it." His voice softened fractionally. "This doesn't concern you, Catherine."

But it does, she wanted to scream. *If it concerns you this much, then it* must *concern me*. But he wasn't going to talk to her about this—even if she asked. And that's what hurt. She couldn't help feeling that this part of himself that he guarded so meticulously had to represent a lack of faith and trust in her.

She might never learn to match Mark's detached attitude regarding their relationship, she told herself bleakly, but she could carefully shield her feelings for him when they were together. He'd made it clear more than once that what he didn't want—or need—was her love.

TEN

Mark threw his pen down onto the desk and leaned back in his chair. Running both hands over his tired face, he swiveled to look out at a gray September afternoon that perfectly matched his mood and allowed the thoughts he'd been unsuccessfully holding at bay to come crashing in.

He was losing Catherine. He could feel her slipping away. Yet he was terrified to reach out, to try to stop her. He feared even that might hasten the inevitable.

The last several weeks had been incredibly frustrating. He'd been more than gratified at how eagerly Beth adjusted to her new home and how easily their lives had settled into a pleasant routine. When the three of them were together they appeared the ideal loving family. It was only when Catherine and he were alone together that he sensed her detachment.

Nightly in their bed Mark tried to break through her reserve to the spontaneous, open woman he knew lay beneath. Oh, she responded sexually—eagerly, even. But something was missing. She subtly deflected his efforts until he'd so completely overwhelmed her senses with passion that she was left no choice but to capitulate. But she always held back a part of herself. Their lovemaking had become a sensual battlefield, and at times he feared she would sense his desperation.

Though he tried to deny it, Mark recognized that his feelings for Catherine were no longer manageable. He couldn't relegate her to some minor corner of his brain to be thought of only when he chose. Not that he'd ever been able to do that, he silently scorned. Holding her at arm's length was becoming frighteningly difficult. He could no longer convince himself that it was merely physical attraction. And he didn't know how much longer he could keep this from her.

The crux of his dilemma was that he couldn't bring himself to completely trust her. The cold, hard fact remained that Catherine had married him for reasons other than himself.

If he had a prayer in hell of binding her to him with love, then he might be safe. But why should Catherine—intelligent, beautiful, educated, and a professional—fall for a man like him? Particularly now that she knew the ugly details of his past—a bastard, who'd grown up on the streets doing less than desirable things simply to survive. Other than great sex and material possessions, he had little to offer a woman like Catherine.

He'd never been very successful, he reflected cynically, in holding the love of a woman. One day she might grow tired of him and simply leave. Hadn't his mother? And his ex-wife? The realization that the pain they had cost him was nothing compared to what was in store should he ever lose Catherine formed a tight knot of panic in his gut.

So why *had* she married him? a tiny voice queried.

That was easy, came the cynical answer—she wanted a child of her own. That was, after all, his part in their bargain. Well, he'd be happy to give her that. That would be one way of binding Catherine to him.

Mark left his chair and went to stand in front of the window, absently studying the pattern of raindrops on the large glass pane.

They'd never gotten around to discussing exactly when she wanted to get pregnant. But she'd left her protection in his hands, indicating that chemical means were out if she was to conceive soon. That must mean that she was considering getting pregnant in the near future. Didn't it? Brutal honesty forced him to admit that sheer gutlessness kept him from broaching the subject now for fear of what she might say.

Damn it, she'd agreed to marry him because she wanted a baby, and so far she hadn't retracted that wish. He tried to convince himself he wasn't above using that bit of logic as all the justification he needed. But the fact that Catherine wanted a child didn't give him the right to unilaterally make that decision for her, subconsciously or otherwise. He'd given her his word that he wouldn't infringe on her autonomy. He'd sworn his respect. No matter how he rationalized his situation, his actions weren't indicative of either.

Still, when a man was desperate, he tended to use desperate measures. He was no closer to a solution now, he realized, than when he'd started.

Catherine couldn't remember wanting—needing—to get home as badly as she did tonight. No, she amended, that wasn't correct. She needed *Mark*. She prayed that she'd find him at the house, that he hadn't been called away tonight of all nights. At the sight of his truck in the drive, a wave of pure relief washed over her, taking with it some of her earlier anguish.

Dashing inside, she went directly to his office. Renewed distress enveloped her when she didn't find him there. Following faint sounds down the hallway, she located him in the kitchen. He looked up from setting the table for two as she walked through the door.

One glance at Catherine's ashen face and Mark knew instantly that something was very wrong. Without thinking, he rounded the table and pulled her protectively against his body.

She seemed to melt into him, not in a sexual manner, but as a wounded animal might, seeking solace. Feeling her shudder, he tightened his hold. "Catherine? What's wrong, honey?" He'd never seen her like this, and it disturbed him in a way that aroused all his protective instincts.

Catherine clung to him for a minute, absorbing his strength before releasing her death grip and easing away from him. "Sorry," she said wearily. "I didn't mean to attack you."

"What's wrong?" Mark repeated, reluctantly letting her go.

Sinking onto a kitchen chair, she wrapped her arms around her waist. "It's been a bitch of a day." She couldn't seem to keep her voice from wobbling.

Mark went to a cabinet and took down a bottle of whiskey. Pouring a generous amount into a glass, he handed it to Catherine. "Drink it."

She complied automatically, almost choking on the fiery liquid scorching her throat. As the whiskey hit her empty stomach, she was immensely grateful for its numbing effect.

Dragging another chair close to hers, Mark straddled it. "Now, talk." This time it was an order.

Her breath soughed unevenly. "I . . . lost a patient today. A little girl. Only six years old. She'd been in a car accident." Her words were given in a jerky monotone, as if delivered by a poor actor reading a script for the first time. "She wasn't wearing a seat belt, and she . . . went through the windshield."

"God, baby." Mark didn't know if he could keep himself from reaching for her, but he sensed she needed to get it all out before she'd accept any comfort.

She made an effort to steady her voice. "She was so small. There wasn't . . . much left of her when they brought her in." Catherine lifted eyes filled with torment to his. "I did all I could," she whispered, the words trailing away into almost nothing, ". . . but it wasn't enough."

He muttered an imprecation. Wrenching his chair aside, he gathered an unresisting Catherine into his arms and carried her up to their bedroom. She was still wearing her surgical scrubs, he noted absently, easing her out of them and into bed. As he tucked the comforter around her, she grabbed his hand, searching his face pleadingly.

"Don't leave me."

"I don't intend to." Hurriedly stripping out of his own clothing, he slid under the covers and cradled her close against himself. For long minutes he merely held her, waiting for exhaustion and the whiskey to take their toll.

But that wasn't what Catherine wanted. "Make love to me, Mark." She heard the urgency in her words and didn't care. Running her hands over his muscled back, she savored the strength contained in him. She needed that strength.

God knew he ached to comply, but he wasn't sure that would be best for her. Raising up on one elbow, he examined the anguish still etched in her features. What she needed was reassurance, and he'd never felt so inadequate in his life. "Honey, you need rest."

"No," she contradicted, pulling his head down to meet her mouth, "I need *you*." She didn't care that she might be revealing things best left concealed. She needed the reaffirmation of life that would come from making love with Mark.

He could feel her desperation. He could taste her urgency. Calling on his dwindling self-control, he lifted his head. "I won't let you blame yourself," he asserted gruffly. "You never give less than your best, and that's all anyone can ask."

"Thank you for that." Tomorrow she would probably appreciate his vehement words, but not tonight. Tonight she craved the sensual oblivion and the potential for life that only Mark could create in her. Restlessly she pressed closer to him.

Mark was acutely aware that tonight she wasn't closing him out. Her responses were spontaneous and open. And vulnerable. A part of him that he thought had ceased to exist long ago cautioned that this time their lovemaking should be different. He didn't question his overriding concern to console Catherine. But rather than their usual fierce, elemental mating, he was overwhelmed with the need to woo her, to take the time to discover and claim every inch of her, and in the process to give them both what they hungered for.

But her seductive movements against him were depleting his resolve. "My way, then," he rasped. "This time it's going to be lingering and thorough." Settling his mouth over hers, he first gentled her, then with his tongue meticulously investigated the taste and texture of her lips before seeking admittance.

Her reaction was instantaneous. Opening her mouth

to eagerly receive his kisses, Catherine gratefully gave herself over to his potent lovemaking.

That he was able to replace her earlier anguish with arousal awakened an unfamiliar yearning in Mark. Her uninhibited response sent the blood racing through his veins to collect in a heated knot low in his groin. But by grim determination he concentrated on slowly pleasuring Catherine. Leaving no part of her body unexplored, he lingered over her, striving with each touch, each caress, to absorb her pain and supplant it with mindless ecstasy.

In the dim twilight he shaped her body with hands that trembled with restrained urgency. Cupping one breast, he stroked its pouting nipple with a calloused thumb, her groaning reaction pushing him closer to the breaking point.

"You have a beautiful body," he whispered hoarsely. Levering himself up on an elbow, he ran passion-glazed eyes over her. And, he concluded distantly, it would be even more beautiful swollen with his child. The idea rocked him. This was the first time he'd ever consciously wanted to create another human being. Never with any other woman. Only Catherine.

But she didn't give him time to dwell on this new revelation. Using hands that shook with passion, she sculpted his hard chest and quivering stomach muscles until she reached his pulsing erection. It was hard and hot and heavy, its strength and size proclaiming his hunger for her. He smelled of it, the dark musky scent of pure sexual arousal, and she gloried in the knowledge that she had at least this much power over him.

Within microseconds his thoughts had splintered. As her hands worked their magic, Mark murmured darkly erotic, almost incoherent, words of encouragement. His own hand moved unerringly to the apex of her thighs, his fingers encountering the slick, sweetly swollen flesh. Catherine made a guttural sound low in her throat. "Mark, please," she pleaded. "I want you inside me . . . now." The urgency of her words snapped the thin thread of his control, and he moved over her, sheathing himself in her in one smooth thrust, then held himself rigid, struggling to come to terms with the overpowering feelings.

"God—so damned good . . ." Much more than physical, she evoked feelings he'd always believed he'd never experience. He was loath to initiate the rhythm that would bring them to release, that would end this incredible sense of oneness they shared. But Catherine shifted under him, and he felt the beginning of her pulsating contractions. That shattered his last-ditch effort to regain control.

"I don't want this to end . . ." he groaned, voicing the elusive yearning. But the spasms had already begun, and there was nothing left to do but give himself up to the conflagration. He was vaguely aware of shouting her name as he emptied himself into her.

He hoped to hell that was all he'd shouted.

He hadn't used anything.

Mark shifted slightly, positioning Catherine more comfortably against his side. She'd finally fallen into an exhausted slumber. He wasn't so fortunate.

Along with the first hint of dawn, his speculation of several days ago came back to taunt him. Had he subconsciously *chosen* not to use protection?

My God, he thought, she could possibly be pregnant now. Hell, he knew her body intimately—better even than his own—and this was approximately the right time in her cycle.

Glancing at Catherine sleeping so serenely, he was

gratified to see that the signs of strain had eased. Because of him, was she going to awaken to a whole new concern?

He ran a free hand through his hair. Could he be that devious? She'd been so vulnerable last night, hurting from the loss of her young patient. And her pain had been so tangible. He'd wanted only to banish it, to comfort her. *She* had wanted that, had demanded it.

Her uninhibited responses, coupled with her need for solace, had stripped away what little control he'd had left. She'd been open and defenseless and needing, and all thoughts of protection had been eclipsed by his desire to console her, to make love to her.

He'd like to crawl out of bed and run, but he wouldn't. Not this time. He'd stay right where he was until she awoke and remembered the events of the night before. And pray that he hadn't made an irrevocable mistake.

Women had been known to hate a man for doing what he'd done, accidentally or not, and the notion panicked him. When had it become so important that he not do anything that might hurt his chances of winning Catherine's love? When had he decided he even wanted her love?

Catherine came awake in slow increments. Something unpleasant nagged at the edges of her consciousness, but she refused to acknowledge it. Instead, she concentrated on the heavily beating heart encased in a very masculine chest that her ear was pressed against. Discovering her husband still in bed gave her a sense of well-being that was astonishing. She knew the exact moment Mark realized she was no longer sleeping.

"How are you?" he asked huskily.

The question brought back the events of the night

before. The pain had thankfully diminished to manageable proportions. It wasn't that she'd never lost a patient before, but no amount of experience made it any less traumatic. Mark's patience and understanding had enabled her to get a grip on her runaway emotions. He'd made her feel safe and secure for the first time in her life. Could he have shown such concern if he didn't care for her much more than he let on?

And his lovemaking. It had been like nothing they'd shared before. His tender consideration of her had made her feel thoroughly loved—almost cherished. Almost.

"Better, thanks to you."

Mark hesitated. "Anything you want to talk about?"

Catherine contemplated the odd undertone in his question. "No, not really. I think we've covered it pretty well."

"Sure?"

She couldn't shake the feeling that they weren't necessarily talking about the same thing. "In med school they told us the best way of handling death is to get it out in the open, then put it behind you. Dwelling on it only . . . prolongs the agony." His arm tightened around her, and she felt his nod.

"If you change your mind, let me know."

Still puzzled, she changed the subject. "Where's Beth?" she asked, suddenly remembering she hadn't seen the child since breakfast yesterday.

"She spent the night with a friend." Throwing the covers aside, he climbed out of bed. "And we need to pick her up. You want to shower first?"

Catherine watched her husband's naked body, a slight frown marring her forehead. "You go ahead. I think I'll lie here a few minutes longer."

He'd been given a reprieve, he thought, his guilt returning full force. Stepping into the shower, he admitted that he was a coward, because he had no intention of bringing up the subject himself. He'd find some way to make this up to her. At the very least he could back off and give her some space.

Well, one thing was damned sure; the guilt eating at him would keep him from brooding over last night's *other* revelation. That his feelings for Catherine ran much deeper than he'd imagined possible.

His only hope was to keep Catherine from discovering it.

ELEVEN

Mark entered the bookstore and headed straight for the section marked Health. He hoped that if this didn't provide answers, it would at least be a distraction.

Waiting for possible repercussions from his slipup that night felt as if the sword of Damocles were hanging above him. Though his plan to give her space was slowly killing him, he'd succeeded in keeping long hours away from home—and Catherine. Coming up with reasonable excuses wasn't easy, but so far he'd managed, as far as he knew, not to raise her suspicions. She was already aware that he was having some problems with his latest project and seemed to accept his absences with little comment.

The long hours and sleepless nights were taking their toll, he reflected as he picked up a particular book and began leafing through it, and exhaustion was a constant companion. That he didn't sleep well without Catherine beside him was another in a long line of undeniable truths being impressed upon him with unrelenting precision. Of course, he had only himself to blame, he thought in derision, for this self-imposed exile from her bed for long stretches of time.

Replacing that book, he picked up another. Returning home at odd hours, he continued silently, supplied the perfect excuse for collapsing, fully clothed, onto the bed in the guest room. It spared him the torture of lying beside his wife and not touching her. He hadn't wanted to disturb her, he'd told Catherine the first time it happened. That she hadn't questioned him left a bitter taste in his mouth and made him discount the flash of pain he thought he'd seen in her eyes. He closed the book with more force than necessary and selected one more.

For the hundredth time he wondered if she was pregnant. He'd planned on merely reducing the number of times they made love, not total abstinence, as it had begun to seem. But because Catherine's hospital hours had recently increased, they rarely slept together, much less made love. Hell, he had no way of knowing whether she'd had her period since that night.

He wasn't certain he could recognize any other early signs of pregnancy. By the time his ex-wife had accidentally become pregnant, he'd been so disillusioned with their marriage that he'd had little inclination, and even less time, to learn about pregnancy.

But with Catherine he yearned to observe every subtle change in her body and to share it with her. Provided she'd let him.

He flipped through his latest selection once more, then, retrieving the first two, headed for the cashier to pay for the three books on pregnancy and childbirth.

"Well, CJ," Lynn Henderson said, busily making notes on her chart, "it appears your dizzy spells are a direct result of being pregnant. Exacerbated, I might add, by working too hard."

Catherine took a minute to absorb the words, her hand moving involuntarily to her stomach. Pregnant. She should have guessed. After all, she was a doctor.

"You're sure?" Catherine asked inanely, then laughed. "Never mind, of course you are."

"You sound surprised," Lynn commented.

"Not surprised really," she said slowly. "It's just that I'm not sure when it happened."

Catherine acknowledged the fact that prophylactics by far weren't the safest method of birth control. Still, Mark had been scrupulous in using protection since their wedding night. In fact, he'd been so thorough that she was beginning to wonder if he were having second thoughts about fathering another child. Especially now that he had permanent custody of Beth.

Lynn looked skeptical. "You haven't been married that long."

"No, we haven't," she answered absently, trying to focus on a nebulous memory teasing at her. Recently their lovemaking had become so infrequent that she'd begun to wonder if Mark was losing interest. Granted, they'd both been extremely busy, yet . . . Abruptly the memory crystallized. Of course! The night her young patient had died. She'd needed Mark so badly, she recalled now with some mortification, that she'd begged— no, *demanded*—he make love to her. And he had, numerous times, with breathtaking tenderness. And without protection.

"If you weren't trying to conceive and succeeded this easily, you're very lucky," Lynn said, closing the chart and dropping it into the file basket on one corner of her desk. "As you well know, women in our age group—no insult intended—occasionally have difficulty." On a sudden afterthought, she added, "You do want this baby, don't you?"

"Oh, yes." Catherine hugged the knowledge close, allowing the joy and growing excitement to permeate every part of her being.

"Then cut back on your hours," she directed sternly. "Get this prescription filled, and I want to see you in a month. Now, go home and tell your husband."

"Yes, Doctor, ma'am," Catherine mocked facetiously. "And thanks." Giving a brief wave, she left her friend's office almost in a daze.

As she opened the door to the Jeep, a new doubt materialized. What would Mark's reaction be? They'd discussed conception only once, and then only superficially. The subject hadn't come up again. Settling behind the wheel, she stared blindly through the windshield, mulling this over.

Though lately Mark seemed to spend more and more time away, when they were together he remained an exquisitely erotic lover, the intensity of their infrequent lovemaking at times bordering on obsession. Whether hers—or his—she was never quite certain. But again she remembered with disturbing clarity that, after that night, he hadn't failed to use protection.

As if the answers might be written there, she studied the concrete wall of the parking deck before her. Yet on the increasingly rare occasions Mark was around, he rushed to help her lift anything heavier than her medical bag, questioned the amount of rest she was getting, and badgered her about her health. She couldn't explain this solicitous concern for her welfare, particularly when he seemed to manufacture reasons to spend so much time away from her. To silence her growing anxiety, she'd once again taken solace in her busy practice, and, in the process, completely ignored the subtle changes occurring within her body.

What was the significance of his contradictory behavior? Of one thing she was certain—his absences couldn't signify infidelity. He had pledged his faithfulness when he'd asked her to marry him. And Mark Garrett, she knew beyond doubt, was a man of his word.

He'd also stated unequivocally that he neither wanted nor needed her love. But that didn't mean, a tiny voice taunted, that he couldn't meet someone else he might care for deeply. They'd never discussed that possibility in any depth. A sad smile tugged at her lips. As she understood all too painfully, humans couldn't always control who they fell in love with.

She rested her forehead against the steering wheel. Something cold darted through Catherine. The thought of Mark denying himself love because of his pledge to her was agonizing.

How *would* he feel about the baby? Would he be glad or feel trapped? Would he accuse her of being careless about birth control? He'd never expressed an interest one way or the other in having a baby. Though he was a wonderful father to Beth, that didn't mean he *wanted* to try fatherhood again.

Why hadn't she considered this sooner? Now was not the time to discover that, to Mark, having a child with her was nothing more than fulfilling his part in their bargain. One hand slid protectively to her still-flat stomach. She already loved the microscopic embryo growing inside her. Mark's child. That Mark might not love and welcome it as well was too painful to contemplate.

Hard on the heels of that bleak thought came another. Heart pounding, Catherine fought for a calming breath. If the glue that held their marriage together was merely physical attraction and sexual chemistry, what would happen to their relationship when her body began changing with pregnancy? When she became ungainly and awkward? When they could no longer have sex?

She gripped the steering wheel until her knuckles whitened. When she'd entered this marriage, she hadn't fully examined all the implications of loving a man who had vowed never to need or want her love. Now more than ever it was important to know where she stood with Mark. What impact would this pregnancy have on their relationship?

But, she reminded herself, Mark could be brutally honest. In fact, she'd come to rely on that honesty. She had no doubt that when she told him, he would let her know exactly where they stood.

Taking comfort, in some convoluted manner, from that thought, she decided nonetheless to wait for the most opportune time to present the news to Mark.

"Dr. Chambers, Dr. CJ Chambers," the nasally intercom intoned for the second time in less than ten seconds, "To ER, stat."

Her mind still clouded with deliberations, Catherine returned her half-finished supper tray and left the hospital cafeteria at a brisk pace. After days of internal debate, she'd finally dredged up enough courage to tell Mark about the baby. If she waited much longer, she lectured silently, he'd be able to figure it out for himself. Her body was already changing faster than she'd anticipated. And intuition told her that he wouldn't appreciate being kept in the dark.

Rounding the corner, she pushed through the broad emergency-room doors and cleared her mind for the task at hand. "Hi, Mary," she greeted the ER nurse, "what've we got?"

"Fourteen-year-old male with a gunshot wound to

the left shoulder. He's being prepped for surgery as we speak.''

"How'd it happen?" Catherine asked as she glanced over the chart.

"A ruckus between two kids that escalated into a shooting," Mary answered in disgust. "Can you believe it?"

"They used to complain about babies having babies. Now we have babies killing babies." A feeling of futility seemed to engulf Catherine and she tried to shrug it away. "Is his family here?"

Mary shook her head. "According to the chart, the kid doesn't have any next of kin. Some man rode in on the same ambulance with him. Apparently he's pretty adamant about being updated on the boy's condition. I haven't talked with him yet."

"Do I have time to speak with him?"

" 'Fraid not, CJ. They'll be ready in OR by the time you're scrubbed and gowned."

Catherine released a quiet sigh. She hated to leave anyone hanging who was waiting for information about a patient. "Tell him that someone will keep him posted and I'll be out as soon as I'm finished," she instructed, heading for the operating suite.

Fortunately, the wound was clean and required only routine repair—if, she thought disparagingly, you could ever consider anything about a gunshot wound to a child routine.

Massaging her tired neck muscles, she crossed the hallway in the direction of the waiting room, hoping she could identify whoever was awaiting word on her patient. Entering, she found a lone figure standing with his back to the door, staring out the window into the darkness beyond. He was dressed all in black leather and even from the back looked dangerous.

As he turned to face her, Catherine stopped dead in her tracks. "Mark? What are you doing here?"

He heard the confusion in her voice before reading it on her face, and steel-cold apprehension raced down his spine. Gut instinct told him he'd made a grave tactical error in waiting. Schooling his features, he walked over to her. "I'm waiting for word on Tiger."

"My patient?" Earlier, she'd paid little attention to her patient's name, much more concerned with his condition and vital stats.

He gave a curt nod. "How is he?"

"He came through surgery fine." Still baffled, Catherine answered by rote. "Luckily the bullet passed between the clavicle and lung and missed the major nerves and blood vessels. The entry and exit wounds were clean. He should be okay in a few days." Her words dwindled away.

Mark released a harsh breath, closing his eyes momentarily in relief.

"You're the man who rode in with him?"

A muscle jerked in his jaw, and again he nodded.

"I don't understand. Why would you be in an ambulance with a child who's been shot?"

Mark hesitated the barest moment. "Because I was there when it happened."

"There? When the shooting occurred?" She couldn't keep the incredulity from her voice.

Shoving the fingers of both hands through his already disheveled hair, he groaned inwardly. "Is there somewhere we can talk?"

Mutely, she led the way to her small office located a few doors away.

Once inside, Mark closed the door, leaning back against it.

"I can't be gone too long," she said, making quick

calls to check on her patient and to leave word where she could be reached. Replacing the receiver, she finally focused on her husband. He looked drawn, she noticed, the black leather jacket seeming to bleach out what color remained beneath his dark tan. "Mark, what's going on?" she asked, not trying to keep the bewilderment from her voice.

From across the room he studied Catherine, taking note of the restrained tension in her. Dressed in surgical scrubs, she radiated a quiet air of proficiency. But the practical clothing didn't detract from the warm, sexy woman he'd come to know was hidden beneath. He wondered if she had any idea what relief and comfort he'd felt when he learned that she was to be Tiger's surgeon. Relinquishing his station against the door, he walked over to the chair in front of her desk and folded his considerable length into it.

"You remember Tiger?"

Catherine nodded, remembering a gangly youth whose street-tough attitude concealed an underlying gentleness.

"I've been working with him. Trying to keep him out of trouble." He laughed bitterly. "As you can see, I haven't been too successful."

"Working with him?" Instead of clearer, things were becoming murkier. "How?"

By strength of will Mark held the keen edge of panic at bay. "Being available when he wants to talk. Trying to get him to see that there's something better in life than membership in the local street gang or breaking the law or doing drugs. Or all of the above."

"Why you? How did you get involved?"

He leaned forward in the chair, propping his forearms on this thighs and pinning her with a penetrating stare.

"I learned about Tiger through my street contacts. Paul sends me others."

She let that sink in for a heartbeat. "Others? How many are we talking about?" She recognized that her agitation was obvious and didn't care.

His answer was slow in coming. "Several."

"Several," she repeated. Shaking her head as if to clear it, she asked with exaggerated calm, "And does your help usually include participating in shootouts?" Catherine shuddered at the violent images forming in her mind's eye.

"No. Not usually." He decided against going into specific gruesome scenarios at the present time.

"This is what all those mysterious phone calls are about," she stated flatly, needing no further confirmation from him. "How long—" her voice dropped to a whisper "—have you been doing this?"

Here it comes, he thought, feeling an invisible fist seize his gut. He ran both hands over his face, then let them dangle between his wide-spread thighs.

"Joe got me involved shortly after he . . . pulled me off the streets. He'd been doing it for God knows how long before that."

The knowledge brought with it a hollow feeling. Very slowly and distinctly she asked, "You mean you've been doing this for years? Long before we married? Or even met?"

"Yes. Look, Catherine," he defended in what he already accepted was no defense at all, "this doesn't concern you."

"Let me see if I understand you correctly," Catherine said carefully, struggling to keep her voice neutral. "You've been helping kids in situations where you put your own life in danger, and it doesn't concern me?"

It was the hurt underlying the bewilderment that most

tormented Mark. He'd never considered that keeping this from Catherine might cause her pain. "Catherine, don't—"

"You don't think you should share something that's obviously this important to you—" she caught her breath at the pain slamming into her "—not to mention dangerous . . . with your wife?"

Her first husband had been an expert at keeping things from her—like the fact he had a lover on the side. If Mark concealed something this important, this integral, what else was he hiding? Did she really know her husband at all?

He'd never considered how Catherine might look at it. Never anticipated his omission might hurt her. *No, you were too damned concerned with protecting yourself.* Guilt made him defensive. "I learned a long time ago not to bare my soul to anyone," Mark said without inflection. "There's a cardinal rule on the streets— don't give away your weaknesses. If you do, it's dead certain you'll regret it."

She steeled herself as new pain assaulted her. He trusted her so little? And if so little trust existed, could their marriage be based on honesty?

The sharp ring of the phone short-circuited the razor-edged thoughts slicing into her mind. A moment later she said in an unnaturally calm voice, "Tiger's out of recovery. He'll be in his room shortly. I'm needed in surgery."

Her dismissive tone chilled him to the core. "This isn't settled."

"No, it's not," she said, pulling a clean white jacket over her soiled scrubs. "All the same, I have to go."

Mark cursed succinctly as full-fledged panic ripped into him, bringing with it the despised feeling of helplessness. He had nothing with which to bind her to him. Certainly not love. Not even a child. While he, came the terrifying realization, was already bound to Catherine on some elemental level he didn't dare name.

_____ TWELVE _____

"Does Mark know where you are?" Steve asked as he joined Catherine on his patio.

"I left a note."

"Ah, I see. And what did the note say?"

Catherine's eyes cut sharply to her friend's face, but she found it difficult to read his expression against the brilliant St. Croix sun. "That I needed time to think."

"And did you tell him where you'd be while you were thinking?" Steve persisted.

She sighed. "Yes. Unlike Mark, I didn't want my spouse to worry." Her sarcasm didn't quite mask the underlying pain.

"Oh, I imagine he'll worry nonetheless. Do you want to talk about it?" Steve asked gently. "It's not like you to go running off into the night, so to speak."

"I need some of your no-nonsense advice." Catherine laughed hollowly and plunged ahead. "Did you know he's set up a foundation to help disadvantaged kids from the inner city? He's on call whenever they need him. Even to the point of putting his own life in danger.'' Her voice held an unmistakable tremor. "But he didn't think I needed to *know* about it."

"And you've decided this signifies what?"

Leaving her lounge chair, she wandered over to grip the concrete railing in the vain hope that it might somehow dispel the pain of her next words. "That he doesn't—can't . . . love me."

"If that's true, then why would your knowing make a difference?"

Startled, she turned the question over in her head but felt far too raw to come up with a definitive answer.

After a few minutes, Steve asked quietly, "Are you going to leave him?"

Leave Mark? She loved him with an intensity that frightened her. How would she survive without him? Her hand settled gently over her womb. And what of the tiny life growing inside her? She'd witnessed the fierce paternal love Mark lavished on Beth and knew he'd love their child just as fiercely. After her own bleak childhood, Catherine could never deny her child that love.

And what of Beth? Catherine had grown to love Mark's daughter as her own. She couldn't desert Beth, not now that she was beginning to shed her timidity and blossom into an outgoing youngster. Not after the many other upheavals in her short life.

"No." It was said in quiet resignation.

"Then shouldn't you be back home in Atlanta?"

"I . . . needed time to sort things out."

"Do you love him?"

She hesitated, then nodded jerkily.

"But it comes with strings," Steve commented in a maddeningly bland voice.

Strings. Was she somehow being unfair to Mark? Something shifted uncomfortably inside Catherine, the heated tropical breeze at sharp variance with the chill suddenly invading her. When love was given, came a nagging query from deep within, shouldn't it be without strings?

Steve crossed the deck to Catherine, tenderly pulling her into a loose embrace and placing a brief kiss on her forehead. "I have a feeling you already know what to do. But consider carefully before making your decision," he cautioned her. "Don't sell Mark Garrett short. Above all, I want to see you happy."

"You're such a dear, dear friend, Steve. Why couldn't I have fallen in love with you?" They both realized the question was rhetorical.

Steve chuckled softly. "Go home, CJ," he said gently. "This isn't where you should be. You're hurting because Mark hasn't said the words, not because he's failed to fill you in on all aspects of his life. Go home and talk to him." Giving her shoulders a squeeze, he went inside the villa, leaving Catherine with her thoughts.

She carefully analyzed Steve's advice. The fact that Mark had never expressed his love didn't mean that it didn't exist. For unlike her father, or her ex-husband, Mark demonstrated his love subtly and often. She'd felt it in his consideration and understanding—experienced it in his exquisite lovemaking. He might not say the words, she acknowledged, but did that make them any less true?

Digesting this possibility, she experienced the ambivalence of fearful hope. She suddenly saw how rigid she'd been by placing all her faith in only one facet of Mark's character—his verbal honesty—and disregarding all others. He might have withheld information about some parts of his life from her, but what exactly did that imply? Was it indeed a critical omission?

Or was it merely an indication of his own insecurity? Could someone who guarded so carefully against her discovering this part of his life *not* care for her, and deeply? Wouldn't Mark have to feel incredibly vulnerable to go to such lengths to conceal this from her?

She was afraid to answer her own questions, afraid she might be giving herself false hope.

And what if he did love her, but could never trust her enough to tell her?

The bottom line was that even if Mark never loved her at all, she could never bring herself to voluntarily leave him.

Though he'd made himself brutally clear, more than once, that love was not to be a part of their relationship, for a brief second she allowed herself to wonder what might happen if she simply told him that she loved him. The answer came quickly. He would withdraw even further into that solitary part of himself he let no one enter, holding her at arm's length until her heart withered and died from the loss. She wasn't sure she could survive. That would be worse in some ways than never seeing him again.

The wrenching pain in the region of her heart reminded her she might well be damning herself to a lifetime of quiet heartache concealing her unwanted love.

Jealousy ate at Mark. He and Beth had arrived at his villa on St. Croix mere hours after Catherine only to learn from the housekeeper that she was with Dalton. It infuriated him. Resting his head against the back of the couch, he welcomed the tranquility of the room and tried to analyze the turmoil tearing at him.

That the friendship between his wife and Dalton had existed long before Mark had entered her life didn't appease him. *He* wanted to be her friend and confidant, the person she sought when hurt or afraid. Like she'd done the night her young patient died. *The night you screwed up*, he reminded himself savagely.

His fury—at himself or the situation he wasn't sure which—was a poor defense against the invading fear.

He'd play it cool. He wouldn't run after her. As if flying all the way from Atlanta to St. Croix didn't count, he mocked himself. And, like the coward he was, dragging Beth along for additional leverage.

Mark ignored the immeasurable feeling of relief that accompanied Catherine's arrival sometime later that afternoon. Hearing her enter the front hallway, he didn't call out to her, waiting instead until she entered the room before speaking.

"Finally decided to pull yourself away from Dalton?" Masking his emotions with cold bravado, he took perverse satisfaction in knowing he'd caught her off guard.

Catherine started in surprise. Whirling around, she found him slouched on the sofa, the fragile wicker a sharp contrast to his tightly leashed power. "Mark!"

"At least you remember my name." Though obviously shocked at finding him there, she exhibited a new confidence. It added to his unease.

"Hello to you, too," Catherine said quietly, ignoring his sarcasm. "What are you doing here?"

He shrugged. "Things aren't settled between us. We need to talk."

"I thought our marriage was built on trust and honesty. What good is talking if you don't say anything?"

Her serenity, considering his own inner turmoil, disturbed him, and a chilling dread settled in his gut. He shifted his attack. "I've never lied to you!"

"Lies are not always by ways of commission. They can be just as much a lie if by omission."

"How much do you need to know?" he asked acidly.

"Why are you so reluctant to share your life with me?" she countered.

Mark's silver gaze sliced her as if trying to see into her soul. He was quiet for so long, Catherine was afraid he wouldn't answer. After interminable moments, he said, "When Elise discovered she was pregnant . . ." He paused. "Well, let's just say she wasn't thrilled about it. The news didn't exactly delight me, either."

Rolling to a standing position, he walked over to gaze blindly out the broad windows. "But after thinking about it a while, I realized the child was as much mine as it was hers. At least I assumed it was." One large shoulder lifted in a shrug, as if that part made little difference. "Even though the marriage was a shambles, there was someone I could do things for, someone I could . . . care about unconditionally. I made the critical mistake of letting Elise know how I felt."

Catherine felt a twinge of apprehension and held her breath, afraid that if she made a sound he might not continue.

"It didn't take her long to figure out that she had a good thing going. All she had to do was threaten to get rid of the baby to bring me to heel. And she used it often—and very effectively."

The words were uglier than Catherine could possibly have imaged, cutting into her heart.

"I finally found a way to bribe her. I offered her a hefty amount of money and an uncontested divorce, if she'd agree to have the baby and give it to me." He laughed bitterly. "You know what happened."

Oh, yes, she knew. After Elise's death, his mother-in-law used emotional coercion to get him to leave Beth with her. And then she, too, tried to take his child from him. Catherine shuddered.

"So you can see how I might be reluctant to tell anyone anything unless there's a real good reason. I give no one a weapon that can be used against me."

And that includes me. She wondered if the pain of that knowledge would cause her knees to buckle.

He turned back to face her, his uneasiness making his anger acute. "What were you planning to do? Leave me because I haven't told you every detail about my life?"

Still trying to absorb what he'd just told her, she was unprepared for his attack. "Mark, I—" But he cut her off.

"And what happens if you're pregnant?" he asked, a knot forming in his belly. Remembering that her first husband had never known about her pregnancy angered him into finally broaching the one subject that he'd evaded for weeks. "Were you simply going to drop out of my life? Or were you planning to quietly get rid of it?"

Catherine sucked in a sharp breath at his outrageous remarks. "Mark, what is it you want from me, from this marriage?"

Like a cornered animal, feeling exposed and vulnerable, he struck out verbally. "You. In my bed, hot and willing," he stated crudely. "Wasn't that our agreement? How else can you get pregnant?" He derived no pleasure from watching the color drain from Catherine's face.

Her hand dropped protectively to her stomach.

Steel glinted in his eyes along with dawning comprehension. "Are you pregnant?"

"It would be a hell of a miracle," she snapped,

using outrage as a shield against his barbed words—
and the guilt pushing at her. "You've barely touched
me in what . . . weeks?"

"No games." His tone was deadly. "Are you
pregnant?"

Catherine's anger dissipated as quickly as it had
come, leaving her defenseless, and for an instant she
didn't, couldn't, conceal the truth.

"You know," he stated, his voice hoarse. "You're
pregnant." For a fraction of a second the wonder and
joy spreading through him overrode his fury. Quickly
closing the space between them, he placed his hand
tenderly over Catherine's abdomen. Caressing. Loving.
Welcoming. His child. His and Catherine's.

The undisguised pleasure on Mark's face almost
broke her heart. "Yes," she whispered, placing her
hand over his.

But an instant later the harsh truth intruded. He
jerked his hand away as if she had become vile. "And
you left without telling me." Something cold and bitter
tore through his gut leaving him raw. He hadn't been
prepared for this betrayal. Not from Catherine. "Now
tell me about honesty." Without giving her a chance
to reply, he strode from the room and out of the villa.

"Mark! Please wait!" Catherine cried, running after
him. But the roar of the van's transmission and the
grinding of gears told her she was too late.

Standing in the dim hallway trying to come to terms
with what had happened, a new realization exploded
inside her head. Even after the way Elise had used her
pregnancy as a cruel weapon against him, Mark had
still trusted Catherine enough to agree to have a child
with her.

Wasn't that ultimate proof of his trust?

And had she, because of her own insecurities, betrayed that trust?

Pivoting quickly, she started for the stairs, stopping abruptly when she discovered Beth sitting forlornly on the third step.

"Beth, honey, what are you doing out here?"

The young girl looked at her accusingly. "You're going away, aren't you?"

"No, honey, I'm not," Catherine said gently, taking Beth's cold hands and warming them with her own.

"Yes, you are." Voice trembling, she tried to hang onto her young dignity. "I heard what Daddy said. Just like you left us and came here," she concluded with childish logic as large tears welled, then spilled down her cheeks. Snatching her hands from Catherine's, she bolted from the house as only a seven-year-old can when running toward something in anticipation—or away from something in desperation.

Suddenly remembering that the dangerous beach stairs out back still hadn't been repaired, Catherine sprinted after her. "Beth! No! The stairs aren't safe!"

Heedless of the warning, the child kept running.

In dread, Catherine watched Beth step onto the wooden landing. Increasing her pace, she prayed she'd be able to catch up with Beth before she started down. "Beth," she screamed again. "Stop! Please let me explain."

Catherine recalled, with grotesque clarity, that the stairs had been treacherous enough the first time she'd used them. Having weathered an unusual season of severe tropical storms, they were now a potentially lethal trap. Holding her breath, she watched Beth place her full weight on the first step. There was the grinding splinter of wood against wood, and the structure swayed sickeningly.

Instinctively Beth grabbed the nautical-rope handrail but continued down the steps. Reaching the landing, Catherine moved gingerly to the edge. Beth was just out of reach. The staircase clung precariously to its mooring, descending the sheer cliff in a drunken, haphazard range that threatened to hurl any unwary trespasser to certain harm on the rocks and sand below. Catherine lunged for the rope handrail, terrified that it might give way. Miraculously it held.

"Grab the rope with both hands, honey," Catherine instructed as calmly as her pounding heart and aching lungs would allow. Beth seized the handrail in a death grip and hung on as, with an ominous groan, the stairs shifted again.

Planting her feet against an outcropping of rock that partially cradled the landing, Catherine fought to control her growing terror and retain her grip on the rope. "I've got you."

She felt the rope bite into the tender skin of her palms, but disregarded the pain. "Very carefully now, one step at a time, I want you to climb back up. Don't let go. Okay?"

Eyes dilated with fear, Beth looked up at her and nodded.

"Good girl." Catherine's palms burned as Beth's weight dragged against the delicate skin. Briefly she debated whether she could attract the housekeeper's attention, but Beth's distress was too acute for any delay in getting her to safety. "Keep going, honey, you're almost there."

Whimpering softly, Beth obeyed. One step. Two.

The searing pain in Catherine's hands was testimony to the child's slow but steady progress. One more step to go. Drawing on a strength fueled by sheer terror, Catherine dragged Beth the last few inches to safety.

"Hush, honey, you're safe now," she said, enfolding the sobbing girl in her arms.

"You won't leave us, will you?" she hiccuped against Catherine's shoulder.

"No, sweetheart."

Beth sniffed softly, struggling to curb her tears. "But you *did* leave." The accusation in the child's words made Catherine's heart hurt.

"You should have given me chance to explain, instead of running away like you did," Catherine chided gently.

"I'm sorry," Beth said in a small voice.

"I needed some time to think. Sometimes grownups have to do that." She hoped the child would accept what was to her a rather lame excuse. "I love you too much to ever leave forever."

Beth hugged her tightly. "I love you, too."

Catherine could no longer ignore the warm stickiness mingling with the steady throbbing in her palms. The rope had broken the skin, and she knew immediate medical attention was imperative.

But Beth was safe. That was all that mattered.

Catherine refused to contemplate the irreparable damage she might have done to her hands in the process.

The antiseptic smell of the hospital made Mark queasy. Or maybe it was the scene he was witnessing. The glaring overhead lights of the examining room left no shadows in which secrets could hide. Vividly revealed to his reluctant view were the ugly abrasions on Catherine's hands. The metallic clatter of surgical instruments against a tray was at odd counterpoint to the heavy beat of his heart.

Catherine's hands. A surgeon's hands. They had well-shaped short nails without the bright polish which had always attracted him in the past. Practical yet feminine, they had been one of the first things he'd noticed about her. He'd come to crave the pleasure and comfort they gave him. And for a second time her hands had been instrumental in saving his daughter.

He prayed that this time the cost was not irreparable.

From across the small examining room, Catherine was acutely conscious of a somber-faced Mark scrutinizing every move Steve made.

"No serious damage done, CJ," Steve said as he finished wrapping her hands in gauze. "They're going to hurt like the dickens for several days, but as long as you keep them from becoming infected, they'll heal with no residual."

Mark didn't wait for Catherine to speak. "You're certain? Shouldn't a specialist look at them?"

"Steve *is* a specialist," she reminded him mildly.

Mark's unconvinced expression didn't falter. "It doesn't matter who or where," he continued, his attention focused on Steve. "Whatever she needs, I'll see that she gets it."

Steve didn't take offense. In fact, he looked very smug, simply smiling and winking at Catherine. "I'm going to let you try to convince your husband that you're okay. I've got other patients who actually do need me." With that announcement he gave her a pat and left the room, pulling the door shut behind him.

"How's Beth?" Catherine asked.

"Fine. They gave her a mild sedative, and I sent her home with Thelma."

"Thank God she wasn't hurt."

As she sat on the examination table, Mark studied her gauze-wrapped hands resting in her lap. "Yeah. Thanks to you. If I hadn't run out like some damned kid, none of this would've happened."

The bitter note in his voice brought her head up with a snap. "Really, Mark, everything's fine. Beth's okay and my hands aren't seriously injured."

Mark didn't respond to her reassurance.

Increasingly uncomfortable under his intense, brooding stare, Catherine attempted to lighten the mood. "Well, I guess this will make me slow down, at least for a while. That should make the obstetrician happy."

Something like anguish darkened Mark's eyes. "Is there a problem with the baby?" He closed the distance between them and, with extreme tenderness, placed his hand over her womb.

She watched the naked emotions flashing across his features. For the first time since she'd known him, he held nothing back. "No, Mark," she said gently. "Really, I'm fine. The baby's fine." She took a deep breath. "And I owe you an apology for not telling—"

"No." His voice held anguish. "Because of my own pettiness, I could have lost Beth. Our child. You." He unconsciously reached for her hands before realizing he couldn't touch them. Instead, he plowed his fingers through his hair.

"Please," Catherine said quietly, "I want to explain."

He nodded once in resignation.

"I've known I was pregnant for only a few days." Had it been such a short time? "If you'll recall, we've both been rather . . . busy lately. I really was going to tell you as soon as we were both in the same room together for more than five minutes." She sighed deeply, looking around the examining room. "I hadn't anticipated breaking the news to you in a hospital."

"After today I wouldn't blame you if you wanted nothing else to do with me." The words sounded as though they were being dragged from him. "The hell of it is that I thought I was being so damned smart.

That if I could just hold myself apart from you, I could insulate myself from pain.''

"You don't have to do this, Mark." The dissipation of the earlier adrenaline surge left Catherine feeling as if all her defenses had been stripped away, and she was afraid she might infer something from Mark's words that wasn't there.

"Yes. I do," he stated flatly. Inhaling deeply, he plunged ahead. "What happened today showed me that no pain is as great as losing to death or injury someone I . . . care about.''

"What are you trying to say, Mark?" she asked quietly, trying to calm the quaver in her stomach.

His jaw ticked convulsively but his gaze didn't waver from hers. "I won't blame you if you didn't give a damn—" he lifted one shoulder, then exhaled "—but I love you.''

Catherine couldn't get a response around the lump in her throat. She knew just how difficult saying those three words had been for him.

"I'm not very good at relationships, but I'll do whatever it takes to keep this marriage together." The statement held the promise of a blood oath.

"You don't have to do this, Mark," she tried to reassure him, aching at the flash of pain she saw in his eyes. "I love you.''

"We can work something out . . ." The words, tinged with pleading, trailed away. "You what?"

"I love you," she repeated and smiled—the first genuine smile in weeks—at his obvious disbelief. "I was afraid you'd never trust me enough to love me."

"It's not you I didn't trust, it was me. Can I hold you?" he asked helplessly.

He sounded so heartbreakingly vulnerable. Catherine quickly slid off the examination table. With exquisite care for her injured hands, Mark enfolded her in his arms.

After a minute he rested his forehead against hers and took a deep breath. "You do understand," he stated quietly, "I'll still continue to work with these kids." There was an underlying plea in his voice. "I'm being as honest as I can with you. I . . . can't give this up." There was a pause. "This is for Joe."

For several heartbeats Catherine remained silent and simply held him, absorbing his desperation and something like resignation. "I won't tell you that it doesn't bother me." She drew back far enough to study his face. "Anything that puts you at risk—" her voice almost failed her "—frightens me. But I do understand that this is part of your life—part of you." She felt tears well in her eyes. "All I ask is that you share it with me."

"That's a promise," he whispered hoarsely, touching his mouth to hers, gently, a solemn gesture that sealed the vow.

All his life he'd been denied love. Because he couldn't bring himself to believe this time was any different, he'd almost pushed away the most precious gift he'd ever been offered. A shudder ran through his body.

"I was certain you could never love me." He swallowed convulsively. "And terrified you'd eventually leave. I figured if I didn't let you know how I felt, if I kept some distance between us, I'd at least have some control over what was happening to me."

She searched his eyes, amazed at his admission. "Why would you think I didn't love you? I thought it was sickeningly obvious."

"Not to me." He smiled wryly. "You kept doing

things that seemed to indicate you didn't think of this marriage as permanent.''

"Like what?" Catherine asked, bewildered.

"You didn't choose to take my name."

"It seemed the most expedient thing to do under the circumstances. You didn't act as if you cared one way or the other." Of course, she now realized, he seldom let people see his true feelings. "What else?"

"You decided to keep your house."

"Only because it represents my first independent act. It had nothing to do with our marriage. If it bothers you," she assured him, "I'll put it on the market as soon as we get back home."

"I think what . . . hurt most," he said, "was that you didn't give me a ring."

She felt tears prick behind her eyes at his simple disclosure. Their inability to open up with each other had caused so much needless pain.

"Oh, Mark," she said gently, holding him as tightly as her bandaged hands would permit, "the reason I didn't give you a ring is because I know from some horrible emergency-room cases what can happen to a man in your line of work who wears jewelry of any kind." She studied his face to make sure he understood. "I was thinking of you when I decided not to give you a ring. I love you, Mark. I have since before we were married."

His mouth clamped over hers roughly, but was tempered with a gentle emotion. He finally seemed to believe her.

When he lifted his head, her face was flushed with arousal—and love. "I hope you have a lot of patience, because you're going to need it to live with me." He studied her a moment. Then he said huskily, "I want to marry you."

Catherine laughed. "We're already married."

"No, I mean a real ceremony—one in a church with Beth there and all the trimmings. And this time"—he kissed her again, hard "—I want a ring."

He looked around the sterile examination room, then back at Catherine. "Can we get out of here? I want to make love to my wife."

They were going to make it, she thought. Now that they'd each trusted enough to declare their love, that love would be strong enough, she was certain, to withstand whatever the future brought.

EPILOGUE

Catherine came awake in the predawn light not certain whether it was the buzzing of the alarm or her husband's exploring hands that had first pulled her from sleep. Moaning softly, she snuggled closer to Mark's strong body and savored the delicious liquid warmth spreading through her.

"We have just enough time." He smiled suggestively, pushing his early-morning erection against the thigh that was draped intimately between his own widespread legs.

Catherine caught her breath, responding to his sensual magic. "And your younger daughter will be up any minute now."

"That's okay," he said, his voice roughened by sleep and arousal. "Beth will take care of Jennifer. She'll love helping her big sister get ready for her art class show."

"And if you want to graduate and get your degree in architecture, you need to study for your last exam—" Her words trailed off into another soft moan as his mouth began a gentle assault on one aching nipple.

219

It was a game, and they both knew how it would end. He laughed huskily as his fingers moved down her body to encounter the proof that she was more than ready to receive him.

The game was over. "What I need . . . is you."

He entered her with exquisite gentleness, filling her with more than just his body. As he began the erotically slow rhythm, he said the words that had become easier for him over the three-plus years of their marriage. He usually chose to tell her when he was deep inside her, like now, when they were as close as a man and a woman could get.

"I . . . love . . . you."

"And I love you," she whispered as the sensual oblivion overtook her.

SHARE THE FUN . . .
SHARE YOUR NEW-FOUND TREASURE!!

You don't want to let your new books out of your sight? That's okay. Your friends can get their own. Order below.

No. 134 ALL BUT LOVE by Ann Howard White
Something about Catherine touched feelings Mark thought he had lost.

No. 71 ISLAND SECRETS by Darcy Rice
Chad has the power to take away Tucker's hard-earned independence.

No. 72 COMING HOME by Janis Reams Hudson
Clint always loved Lacey. Now Fate has given them another chance.

No. 73 KING'S RANSOM by Sharon Sala
Jesse was always like King's little sister. When did it all change?

No. 74 A MAN WORTH LOVING by Karen Rose Smith
Nate's middle name is 'freedom' . . . that is, until Shara comes along.

No. 75 RAINBOWS & LOVE SONGS by Catherine Sellers
Dan has more than one problem. One of them is named Kacy!

No. 76 ALWAYS ANNIE by Patty Copeland
Annie is down-to-earth and real . . . and Ted's never met anyone like her.

No. 77 FLIGHT OF THE SWAN by Lacey Dancer
Rich had decided to swear off romance for good until Christiana.

No. 78 TO LOVE A COWBOY by Laura Phillips
Dee is the dark-haired beauty that sends Nick reeling back to the past.

No. 79 SASSY LADY by Becky Barker
No matter how hard he tries, Curt can't seem to get away from Maggie.

No. 80 CRITIC'S CHOICE by Kathleen Yapp
Marlis can't do one thing right in front of her handsome houseguest.

No. 81 TUNE IN TOMORROW by Laura Michaels
Deke happily gave up life in the fast lane. Can Liz do the same?

No. 82 CALL BACK OUR YESTERDAYS by Phyllis Houseman
Michael comes to terms with his past with Laura by his side.

No. 83 ECHOES by Nancy Morse
Cathy comes home and finds love even better the second time around.

No. 84 FAIR WINDS by Helen Carras
Fate blows Eve into Vic's life and he finds he can't let her go.

No. 85 ONE SNOWY NIGHT by Ellen Moore
Randy catches Scarlett fever and he finds there's no cure.

No. 86 MAVERICK'S LADY by Linda Jenkins
Bentley considered herself worldly but she was not prepared for Reid.

No. 87 ALL THROUGH THE HOUSE by Janice Bartlett
Abigail is just doing her job but Nate blocks her every move.

No. 88 MORE THAN A MEMORY by Lois Faye Dyer
Cole and Melanie both still burn from the heat of that long ago summer.

No. 89 JUST ONE KISS by Carole Dean
Michael is Nikki's guardian angel and too handsome for his own good.

No. 90 HOLD BACK THE NIGHT by Sandra Steffen
Shane is a man with a mission and ready for anything . . . except Starr.

No. 91 FIRST MATE by Susan Macias
It only takes a minute for Mac to see that Amy isn't so little anymore.

No. 92 TO LOVE AGAIN by Dana Lynn Hites
Cord thought just one kiss would be enough. But Honey proved him wrong!

No. 93 NO LIMIT TO LOVE by Kate Freiman
Lisa was called the ''little boss'' and Bruiser didn't like it one bit!

Meteor Publishing Corporation
Dept. 393, P. O. Box 41820, Philadelphia, PA 19101-9828

Please send the books I've indicated below. Check or money order (U.S. Dollars only)—no cash, stamps or C.O.D.s (PA residents, add 6% sales tax). I am enclosing $2.95 plus 75¢ handling fee for *each* book ordered.

Total Amount Enclosed: $_____.

____ No. 134	____ No. 76	____ No. 82	____ No. 88
____ No. 71	____ No. 77	____ No. 83	____ No. 89
____ No. 72	____ No. 78	____ No. 84	____ No. 90
____ No. 73	____ No. 79	____ No. 85	____ No. 91
____ No. 74	____ No. 80	____ No. 86	____ No. 92
____ No. 75	____ No. 81	____ No. 87	____ No. 93

Please Print:
Name _____
Address _____ Apt. No. _____
City/State _____ Zip _____

Allow four to six weeks for delivery. Quantities limited.